Praise for Christine McGuire's Novels of Suspense

UNTIL WE MEET AGAIN

"A great legal thriller . . . that allows readers to see [Kathryn] as a mom, a woman, and an attorney. . . . A fascinating and complex tale."

—Barnesandnoble.com

UNTIL THE BOUGH BREAKS

"A provocative story examining the ugly twists of domestic violence . . . sharp legal thriller."

—*Publishers Weekly*

UNTIL DEATH DO US PART

"A gripping drama. . . . Readers are treated to three-dimensional human beings filled with fears, doubts, and flaws."

—Amazon.com

UNTIL JUSTICE IS DONE

"What sets McGuire's novels apart from the pack is the level of realism she brings to the legal aspects of the story."

—*The Sentinel* (Santa Cruz, CA)

UNTIL PROVEN GUILTY

"A tense, nerve-jangling thriller that should satisfy fans of *The Silence of the Lambs*."

—Peter Blauner, bestselling author of *The Intruder* and *Slow Motion Riot*

Books by Christine McGuire

Perfect Victim
Until Proven Guilty
Until Justice Is Done
Until Death Do Us Part
Until the Bough Breaks
Until We Meet Again
Until the Day They Die

For orders other than by individual consumers, Pocket Books grants a discount on the purchase of **10 or more** copies of single titles for special markets or premium use. For further details, please write to the Vice President of Special Markets, Pocket Books, 1230 Avenue of the Americas, 9th Floor, New York, NY 10020-1586.

For information on how individual consumers can place orders, please write to Mail Order Department, Simon & Schuster, Inc., 100 Front Street, Riverside, NJ 08075.

Christine McGuire

UNTIL *the* DAY THEY DIE

POCKET STAR BOOKS
New York London Toronto Sydney Singapore

The sale of this book without its cover is unauthorized. If you purchased this book without a cover, you should be aware that it was reported to the publisher as "unsold and destroyed." Neither the author nor the publisher has received payment for the sale of this "stripped book."

This book is a work of fiction. Names, characters, places and incidents are products of the author's imagination or are used fictitiously. Any resemblance to actual events or locales or persons, living or dead, is entirely coincidental.

An *Original* Publication of POCKET BOOKS

A Pocket Star Book published by
POCKET BOOKS, a division of Simon & Schuster, Inc.
1230 Avenue of the Americas, New York, NY 10020

Copyright © 2001 by Christine McGuire

All rights reserved, including the right to reproduce this book or portions thereof in any form whatsoever. For information address Pocket Books, 1230 Avenue of the Americas, New York, NY 10020

ISBN: 978-1-4767-9694-9

First Pocket Books printing April 2001

10 9 8 7 6 5 4 3 2 1

POCKET STAR BOOKS and colophon are registered trademarks of Simon & Schuster, Inc.

Front cover illustration by Lisa Litwack, photo credits: top, Christopher Wadsworth/Photonica; bottom, Paul Mason/Photonica

Printed in the U.S.A.

ACKNOWLEDGMENTS

With deep gratitude to
my literary agent
Richard Pine
and my editor
Jason Kaufman

This book is lovingly dedicated
to the memory of

Arthur (Artie) Pine

our agent and friend

Christine & Richard

Prologue

"How long has he been like this?" the woman asked, sitting on the edge of the motel bed.

"I don't know, exactly." He lit a Marlboro and sat in the only chair. He aimed the remote at the television and muted the sound, but continued watching the movie. It was the original, uncolorized version of The Wild Ones.

"What do you mean, you don't know? How long ago did you check him last?"

"No more than a couple of hours."

"A couple of hours! Goddammit! I told you to check him every fifteen minutes. What happened?"

"I fell asleep. I called you as soon as I woke up and checked him," he told her, then added, "And don't get hysterical, that sure as hell won't help anything."

"You idiot," she muttered, then leaned over, placed her ear on the rapidly rising and falling chest, and listened intently, motioning for the man to be quiet.

"Just our luck. What's wrong with him?" he asked without diverting his eyes from the TV.

"I'm not sure, but he can barely breathe. His lungs are congested, and his lips and fingernails have turned blue."

"Do something."

"I can't do anything. It may already be too late, but we've got to take him to the hospital."

"Don't be stupid, you know we can't do that. Now, do something before . . ."

On the bed, labored breathing deteriorated into jagged, desperate gasps, followed by wet gurgles as spittle and reflux were sucked deep into the lungs. He struggled briefly, then expelled his final breath. It sounded like a sigh, like he was relieved to give up the futile battle for breath, and life.

Then, his arms and legs convulsed once, his face turned pale and he lay still.

"My God, oh my God! Jesus, he quit breathing!" The woman groaned. "Breathe into his mouth while I do chest compressions!"

"I ain't puttin' my mouth over some stiff's."

She looked up. "If you don't start mouth-to-mouth right now, I swear to God, I'll kill you."

He shrugged and bent over and covered the inert body's mouth with his own, blowing in air.

After fifteen minutes, she stopped the chest compressions. He laughed and sat down in the chair, leaned back, propped his feet up on the writing table with his ankles crossed, and lit a Marlboro.

Her eyes filled with tears, and she trembled uncontrollably. "He's dead. What are we going to do?"

"We're going to bury him."

"We can't just walk into a funeral parlor off the street and have him buried, you sonofabitch," she shouted. "They'll ask questions."

"Who said anything about a funeral parlor?"

1

SANTA RITA, CALIFORNIA
MISSION HEIGHTS
TUESDAY, 2:30 A.M.

"Turn off the headlights, this is the street," the big man in the right front seat ordered. "Go slow and don't use the brakes, we don't want the brake lights to go on."

The driver turned and idled the new black Chevy Suburban up the street.

"Stop here."

The driver steered to the shoulder of the narrow street, applied the emergency brake, and switched off the ignition.

The husky front seat passenger and the short woman in the rear seat each wore black trousers and turtlenecks, with identical new, black size twelve Nike sneakers.

The big man smeared face-black over his exposed skin and handed the jar to the woman, who did the same. Then, they slipped on black leather gloves and pulled dark ski masks over their faces.

The front seat passenger grabbed a tool pouch, a

length of polyvinyl rope, and a sling from behind the seat. The sling was tied to a canvas bag about a foot in diameter and two feet long, with a drawstring closure at the top. It was lined with a plastic trash bag.

He set the gear on the floorboard between his feet, and quickly inventoried the contents of the tool pouch: two cans of pepper-spray dog repellant; a sealed, plastic Ziploc food-storage bag containing a liquid-impregnated washcloth; several specialized hand tools and supplies; a black Mini-MagLite; and a .25 caliber Baretta automatic with a baffled silencer screwed into the barrel.

He turned and looked over the seat. "Ready?"

The woman nodded. "How will we know the right room?"

"I've been watchin' the fuckin' place for three days, stupid. Now let's go." He turned to the driver. "Fifteen minutes, max. If anything happens, or we're not back in fifteen minutes, take off. You remember where to rendezvous if we get separated?"

The driver nodded, then checked the door-actuated dome light, from which the bulb had previously been removed. "No sweat, nothin'll go wrong." The big man raised his sweater, made sure his pager was set to vibrate, and hooked it back inside his waistband next to his skin.

"Okay, let's go."

He cautiously opened the passenger door and climbed out, hung the coiled rope and sling over one shoulder and the tool pouch over the other, then walked to the rear of the vehicle to open the double doors.

The woman crawled out the rear of the van, dragging a fiberglass extension ladder. She checked the deserted street, stuck an arm through the ladder and lifted it in the crook of her arm.

They walked silently up the sidewalk, turned into the driveway, then crouched and sprinted the final twenty uphill yards along the hedge that bordered the drive's west side, stopping when they reached the overhang of the detached three-car garage.

They squatted on their haunches and leaned against the garage, facing the kitchen window of the house across a four-feet-wide breezeway, gulping deep breaths of air through their mouths while they listened for sounds of human or animal activity. A dog barked in the distance and a few frogs croaked. A soft breeze rustled the leaves of the old oak trees that isolated the property from its nearest neighbors, but no sound came from inside the house.

After several minutes, the big man stood and motioned for his partner to follow. They swung open the wooden gate that connected the garage to the house, and crept down the concrete walkway, around the corner, and across the open lawn of the dark yard.

The woman stuck the ladder's hinged rubber feet in the soft flower bed, working them around until they were firmly planted, extended the steps, and leaned the top of the ladder against the house. Wrapped with old towels, the rails came to rest silently on the exterior wall.

The large man climbed up the ladder far enough

to peer through the second-floor window. A soft night light provided sufficient illumination to confirm that what they intended to steal was in the room.

He removed his right glove, reached under his sweater, and pulled two large safety pins from a shirt pocket, which he stuck between his lips to hold, then located two wires emanating from the bottom of the window screen. He gently pulled the two wires away from the screen with a metal nut pick, stuck one pin through each, and fastened the pin heads. He retrieved a small battery-powered RadioShack Multimeter from his bag and touched a test probe to each safety pin. He nodded as the needle on the softly backlit meter swung over to register a low-level voltage, confirming that the wires connected the screen to a central alarm system.

The man on the ladder wiped sweat from his upper lip with his sweater sleeve, through the mouth opening of the ski mask. He uncoiled a short length of small-gauge black wire with alligator clips on the ends, and clamped each clip firmly to a safety pin.

With the makeshift jumper maintaining the electrical continuity of the alarm circuit, normally provided by tiny conductors embedded in the screen mesh, he severed the original wires with diagonal cutters.

He paused briefly to be sure no audible alarm was triggered, then pulled a Stanley utility knife from the tool pouch, and sliced a U-shaped opening around the lower perimeter of the aluminum screen frame. He rolled up the mesh flap, secured it in place with three old-fashioned wooden clothespins, reached inside to release several spring-loaded latch pins and lifted out the screen.

He indicated to his partner on the ground that the window was ajar by forming a circle with his thumb and forefinger, meaning he wouldn't need the glass cutter.

Silently, he slithered headfirst into the room. Moments later, he stuck his head and shoulders out the window, lifted the sling and now-full bag over the ledge, and lowered them with the rope. As soon as the bag was secure in the hands of his partner, he backed out the window and scrambled down the ladder carrying the tool pouch.

When they climbed back into the Suburban, the big man tossed his ski mask and the bag with its valuable contents on the rear seat beside his partner.

"Get the fuck outta here," he told the driver, "before this damn thing starts makin' noise."

2

Amber lights flashed atop the police barricades that blocked the entrance to the narrow street, so the red BMW idled past and nosed into the curb on Juan Cabrillo Avenue. The driver climbed out and locked the doors, then dropped the remote into a black handbag slung over her right shoulder. Although she wore Liz Claiborne jeans and an indigo blue T-shirt under a black leather jacket, she was immediately recognized as the District Attorney by the uniformed deputy assigned to secure the intersection.

"Good morning, Ms. Mackay," the deputy greeted her.

"Good morning, Deputy Alvarez," she answered, glad the patrol deputies wore nameplates.

The deputy pointed her up the street to a driveway, which was cordoned off by yellow crime scene tape stretched between hedgerow borders.

She strode quickly up the hill and ducked under the tape into the secured area. A trailer-mounted, gas-powered generator on the lawn strained to supply power to a bank of spotlights at the top of its collapsible power pole, which cast surreal shadows through the wet fog. Lights blazed from every room of the house, which Mackay guessed numbered a dozen or more.

When her eyes adjusted, Mackay spotted Sheriff's Chief of Detectives Granz and Crime Scene Investigation Unit Sergeant Yamamoto standing near the front door of the house, talking, and walked across the damp grass to where they stood.

"Good morning, Dave, Charlie," she greeted them.

A man of few words, Charlie Yamamoto smiled politely and nodded but didn't say anything. He bent down and picked up his camera case, then turned and headed toward the backyard, through a gate where another investigator was hunched over inspecting it and the adjacent garage wall.

Granz turned. "What are you doing here, Kathryn?"

"County Communications notified me. Is that a problem?"

"It is until I know what's happening."

"Protocol requires them to call."

"Protocol says when it's my investigation, it's my decision." He shrugged. "Forget it, you're already here."

"Fill me in on what's been done so far."

He stared at her for several seconds before answering. "Patrol secured the house and called out detectives. Yamamoto and his CSI unit got here about an hour ago."

"Has the house been processed?"

"Not completely, we haven't had time, and the grid search just got under way. I sealed off the nanny's private quarters that adjoin the bedroom."

"Neighbors?"

"Detectives are going door-to-door."

"What's gone out over the air?"

"County Comm broadcast a county-wide BOLO within minutes," he told her, referring to a Be-On-the-Lookout-For bulletin. "Protocol, you know? We got out a regional teletype immediately."

"How about entering the name in the National Crime Information Center's missing persons registry?"

Granz drew in a deep breath and expelled it audibly and forcefully. "Already done, Kathryn. And the Sex Crimes Unit's checking names, addresses and MOs of registered offenders in the area."

Kathryn nodded. "Have you called DOJ?" Mackay asked. DOJ was law enforcement jargon meaning the California Department of Justice, whose criminalists assisted law enforcement on complex crime scenes.

"Dammit, CSI's on top of things. If I need DOJ's help, I'll call 'em," he answered testily. "Are you afraid we can't handle this?"

A knot formed in the pit of Mackay's stomach, as it often did lately when she and Granz interacted. Although she wouldn't have hesitated to answer the challenge a few months earlier, she resisted her first impulse. Instead, she flashed back a couple of years, to a time when she and Dave worked together side by side prosecuting murders and rapes; she as an assistant DA, and he as the senior DA inspector. They were an effective team, their professional lives meshing smoothly with their romantic relationship.

Until a year or so ago, when events led Granz to have an affair with a woman named Julia Soto, and Mackay to end her relationship with him as a result.

Shortly after she became DA, he resigned to accept his current position. His move, however, had not entirely defused the tension between them.

Kathryn lay her hand on his arm. "Of course not. When you're in charge, I know everything will be done right. It's just that . . ."

He removed her hand, but said, "Sorry, I shouldn't have said that."

"Apology accepted. Now, could you walk me through the crime scene? It's cold standing still."

He looked at her briefly before answering, then finally said, "Sure."

He turned and motioned her to follow him toward an opening between the garage and the house where an investigator was waving a high-intensity, hand-held lamp slowly back and forth over a head-high gate. Mackay recognized the instrument as a Woods Lamp, which could detect minute particles of material too small to be seen by the naked eye, even in bright sunlight. He stopped to allow them to enter the breezeway between the garage and house, then went back to work.

"Looks like they entered the backyard through this gate," Granz explained. "CSI's hoping it snagged a few threads of fabric off their clothing when they went through, but so far it doesn't look like it."

"They?" Mackay asked.

"Yamamoto says there were two sets of shoe tracks. He's getting ready to photograph them."

"He can't cast them?"

"They're just impressions left on the damp grass. He says he needs more pronounced three-dimensional impressions to pour casting material."

When they reached the corner of the house where the breezeway and flagstone path ended, Charlie Yamamoto was hunched over with his camera case open, positioning an 18-inch ruler beside one of the shoe prints, which was already fading as the dew on the grass dried.

"Can you still photograph them, Charlie?" Mackay inquired.

Yamamoto didn't look up. "Got to."

He positioned a tripod over the print, mounted a manual Nikon, then lay a flashlight on the ground and aimed the beam across the top of the print. "Oblique lighting. Increase contrast, improve visibility."

He focused, snapped several frames, adjusted the focus and exposed several more. Then he stepped back and nodded to himself, and repeated the process on a second print. "Same shoe, same size, but two people."

"How can you tell?" Mackay wanted to know.

"Gait characteristics—stride lengths, step lengths, foot angles, walking base all different. One big person, one not so big. Maybe a man and a woman."

"You think they're examination-quality photographs?" she asked, hoping he'd confirm they would be sufficiently detailed to allow forensic examination.

"Good enough to ID class characteristics—size and shoe design—eliminate ninety-nine-point-nine percent of the two billion pairs of shoes in U.S. Probably not enough for positive ID of specific shoes. Look brand new."

"How do you establish the size and brand?"

Yamamoto sighed and looked at the District Attorney. "Depends. Book called *Sole Source* has big list. FBI footwear design database has thousands. I submit photos, they compare. Voilà."

Mackay nodded. "Thanks."

Yamamoto returned his attention to his camera. "Talk too much, never get anything done," he mumbled to himself.

Having worked with the investigator for many years and greatly appreciating his expertise, Mackay and Granz knew when to leave him to his work.

They surveyed the rear yard, whose landscape architecture comprised multilevel terraces to create an illusion of an expansive space, although it was not large. A gentle stream of water emanated from under the dining room, tumbled over strategically placed rocks, curved under an arched footbridge, and cascaded into an elevated spa. Water from the spa spilled into the main pool, which was lighted by an underwater fiber-optic system, and featured a vanishing edge at the rear, which implied that the water went on infinitely.

The walking surfaces surrounding the pool and

spa were Rocky Mountain quartz. Lounging areas were broken into small intimate enclaves furnished with modern patio furniture. A free-standing element at the rear of the pool housed a barbecue, flagstone fireplace, restrooms and showers.

"It looks like a park," Mackay said.

"Life is good," Granz observed.

"I wonder if the owners would agree right now, under the circumstances," Mackay mused.

Although it was no longer necessary in the increasing dawn light, he shined his flashlight to the left of the deck, where a yellow fiberglass extension ladder leaned against the exterior wall, its feet hidden among a profusion of petunias and pansies. The top rails were wrapped with white cloth, and rested beside an open second-story window.

"CSI located the window screen on the lawn. It was cut, then removed. They'll seize the ladder as soon as they've photographed it. Won't do any good as evidence, though."

"Why not?"

"I asked the same question. Yamamoto looks at me and says, 'Ordinary ladder. Brand new. Thousands of 'em sold everyplace—Ace Hardware, Home Depot, you name it. Ladders got no serial numbers you know. Waste of time!' "

Mackay shrugged. "I suppose it'd just slow them down getting away. Was the house alarmed?"

"Yeah." He aimed the flashlight at the window, where two small wires dangled over the ledge. "Silent, hardwired system monitored by First Alarm's central computer through telephone lines."

"Did it go off?"

"No, the perps bypassed it with a couple of safety pins and a circuit bridge. Simple, but effective."

Kathryn thought for a minute. "They must have driven up here. They wouldn't have carried that ladder very far on foot. Maybe there's been prior criminal activity, or Patrol Fled a suspect in the area. Is someone checking?"

Other than a heavy, exasperated sigh, Granz didn't react. "One of my analysts is searching all field interrogation cards and incident reports as we speak. We're running raps on the parents, too. We closed off the street all the way down to the Juan Cabrillo Avenue intersection," he told her. "CSI searched along the edge of the pavement. The shoulder along there is soft dirt. They found a tire track."

"Good enough to cast or photograph?"

"Don't know, but we can check."

As they rounded the end of the hedge, a blond woman looked up and held out her hand. "Careful, Lieutenant, Ms. Mackay, I've got a viable tire tread impression. We've taken photographs, now I'm going to cast it."

They walked around and stood behind her, watching her prepare a bucket of 8,000 psi dental stone. She mixed it until the powder and water were a liquid consistency, then carefully poured the mixture into a 36 inch section of the track, completely filling the indentation.

While she waited for the dental stone to set so it could be lifted, she told them, "This was left by a full-size pickup truck, Jeep, Land Rover, or something similar. The tire size is too big for a passenger car, and the tread pattern is consistent with a heavy-duty vehicle."

"How much do you think they'll tell us?" Mackay wanted to know.

"The class characteristics will indicate if they were OE tires or—"

"OE?"

"Original equipment. If so, that narrows the vehicle possibilities considerably. The tires appear to be new, but even a few miles of driving causes tiny cuts, nicks and abrasions that we can match to the tires that caused them, and place the car at the scene." She paused, then added, "Assuming it's located."

"Yeah, assuming." Granz flipped off his flashlight and peered into the early morning sky. "It's getting light enough for the chopper to go to work with infrared and heat-detecting equipment. The pilot's spinning it up now."

"What about dogs?"

"We called in civilian search-and-rescue units, including that guy with the bloodhounds. The more time passes, the more we need his hounds. They have sixty times the tracking power of the German Shepherds in our canine units. Now, why don't we go in the house. Detective Miller's inside with Garrett and Gayle Alexander."

"Let's do," Mackay agreed. "Maybe the parents can help us figure out what happened to their baby daughter."

3

Entry to the Alexander home was gained through huge beige double doors with highly polished brass hardware. The entryway was accented by a glass border that rose vertically, then arched majestically over the doors in concentric circles of cut glass mounted in narrow brass ribs.

The vestibule was about thirty feet square, with shiny beige slate floor tiles. Immediately inside, a chocolate trimmed, off-white Persian rug supported a glass-top table and an incongruous fall plant arrangement. Although there was no physical barrier, two white marble columns demarcated the imaginary boundary between the foyer and the living room, and supported a two-story high, steeply arched ceiling. A brass and frosted glass chandelier hung from the apex and cast indirect light upward, which reflected back into the room.

To the left was a sitting area, sparsely furnished

with a single indirectly lit abstract painting, a glass-top table with four beige upholstered chairs, and two glass curio cabinets. It adjoined a wide, carpeted stairway whose top landing was not visible from the ground floor.

The entire large living room, however, could be observed from the foyer, between the marble columns. It was finished with beige plaster walls and plush off-white carpeting, high ceilings and a natural oak-framed fireplace with a marble hearth.

Gayle Alexander leaned against the arm of an upholstered sofa behind a square glass-top table, feet tucked up under her right hip, arms across her chest and straight blond hair falling over her shoulders. Her startlingly blue eyes were wide open and alert, albeit somewhat puffy, and she wore a white terry cloth robe with SQUAW VALLEY USA embroidered above five interlocking Olympic rings on the left breast. An empty cup perched on her lap.

Garrett Alexander slouched beside her, holding one of her hands in both of his. He wore faded jeans, a blue chambray shirt and Fila thongs. His sandy brown hair was mussed, but he appeared organized and calm except that behind his wire-rimmed glasses his blue eyes also looked red and raw.

Granz turned to Mackay. "I'll take the lead, Kathryn. Agreed?"

"No problem," she assured him. "It's your investigation until you turn it over to my office."

Detective James "Jazzbo" Miller sat in an overstuffed chair talking to the Alexanders. When he saw his boss and Mackay, he stood and motioned them to join him. Miller was tall, overweight, red-headed with a ruddy complexion, a full beard, and a perpetual smile that displayed tobacco stained teeth. His nickname derived from his avocation as a trombonist in a local jazz combo. "Mornin' Ms. Mackay. Mornin' Lieutenant," Miller greeted them, then turned to the Alexanders. "Mr. and Mrs. Alexander, this is Lieutenant David Granz, the Sheriff's Chief of Detectives, and Kathryn Mackay, the District Attorney."

Both extended their hands, then motioned to Granz and Mackay to sit on the smaller sofa across from the table. Miller resumed his position in the chair, and drew their attention to a Panasonic mini-recorder on the table.

Granz slid forward on the sofa and clasped his hands. "We are going to do everything possible to find your baby. Right now, we need to ask you some questions and record your answers, if you don't mind."

"Go ahead," Garrett Alexander told them.

"Some of the questions may be difficult, but I assure you they're absolutely necessary. The first few hours are most critical, so we need to get as much information as possible, as quickly as we can."

"What do you need to know?" Mrs. Alexander asked.

"Start by telling us exactly how you learned that Janey was missing," Mackay suggested.

Gayle Alexander placed her feet flat on the floor, set her cup on the table, and sat up ramrod straight, then drew in a breath that caught in her throat. "I . . . we get up very early for work on weekdays, so Addie, our nanny, usually takes care of Janey's nighttime feeding. She came to the master bedroom and woke me at about five after three this morning to ask if I had taken the baby for her feeding. I said no. Then she told me she couldn't find Janey."

"You said, 'I,' " Mackay interjected. "Was your husband gone?"

"Addie speaks Spanish," she explained. "Garrett isn't bilingual."

Granz nodded.

"Well, we ran down the hall to the nursery, but Janey wasn't there. When Garrett noticed the open window and missing screen, he looked outside and saw the ladder, and called nine-one-one. I found the note in the crib."

"The note?" Granz asked.

Garrett Alexander withdrew a folded sheet of pink paper from his back pants pocket and held it for several seconds before handing it to Granz. "It says not to get the police involved, but our only chance of getting Janey back is working with you."

Granz carefully lay the note on the coffee table and removed a roller ball pen from his shirt pocket, with which he unfolded and smoothed the creases in the eight-by-ten, pink sheet of copier paper. Mackay slid close to Granz but, realizing their thighs were touching, moved away slightly, then read the note aloud.

"StaY neAr yOUr pHoNe And dont cALL cops! you WILL BE cOnTACted ABouT RanSOM fOllOw InSTRucTIONs eXactlY 2 sEE BAby aLIVe."

"Cutouts from newspapers and magazines," Mackay observed. To herself, she thought *The only prints we're likely to find on the note now are the Alexanders'.*

Granz removed a flat plastic evidence bag from his briefcase and slid it carefully over the note, then sealed the bag, initialed the seal, and placed it into his briefcase. "I'll have the DOJ lab examine this right away." Then he turned to Garrett Alexander.

"Has anyone contacted you claiming to be the kidnapper?"

"No."

"How many phone lines come into your home?"

"Four."

"Why so many?"

"One business, one personal, and a dedicated line for each of our computers. Sometimes we telecommute."

"What sort of work do you do?"

"Software development," Garrett Alexander answered.

"You work for the same company?" Mackay asked.

"No, different companies in the same industrial complex in Cupertino."

Granz turned off the recorder and turned to Miller. "Jazzbo, have the phone company install tracing and trapping equipment on all lines, now. And have CSI put recorders on them, then assign a detective to monitor the lines continuously."

When Miller left, Granz switched the recorder back on, and told the Alexanders, "Beginning now, don't answer any phone calls until one of my detectives tells you to."

"What if the kidnapper refuses to talk with your detective?"

"The kidnapper won't know the detective is on the line," Mackay assured them. "The caller will believe he's talking just to you. Lieutenant Granz and his detectives are experts at handling situations like this. The best way to bring Janey home quickly is to follow their advice."

Mackay paused, then asked, "Do either of you have any idea who might take your baby, or why?"

Garrett Alexander answered. "No."

Granz waited for more, but nothing came. "Okay. Are either of you involved in a secret software project, or something that makes you vulnerable to extortion?" he finally asked.

"No."

Granz arched his eyebrows. "You're sure?"

"In software development, age thirty is ancient. We're managers," Gayle explained.

"How about layoffs, union issues or other labor problems?"

"No."

Granz changed directions. "Does Jane have any scars, physical deformities, or other identifying marks?"

Gayle grasped the collar of her robe, which had fallen open, and glanced at her husband, who closed his eyes, then opened them slowly to indicate his assent.

"A birthmark."

"Could you describe it?"

Rather than answer, Gayle reached into her robe pocket, hesitated, pulled out a Polaroid color print, gazed at it for a moment, then handed it to Granz.

Granz felt her body warmth in the photograph. The infant was lying on her back in a shallow tub of soapy water, shampoo in her hair and a yellow rubber duck clutched in her left hand. A man's hand, which he assumed was Garrett Alexander's, held Jane's head up out of the water. Only the upper torso was visible, but Granz needed no further description of the birthmark. A large, angry-looking strawberry hemangioma covered the entire left side of the infant's tiny chest, tapering from the full width of the left collarbone to a stubby point just above the navel. It was shaped like a grotesque, off-center, slanted mushroom.

Granz swallowed hard. "Can you please describe the clothing she was wearing when she went to bed?"

Gayle answered. "A pink and white gown with drawstrings on the bottom over a white T-shirt and diaper. When she's dressed, she looks normal." She flushed, embarrassed for sounding apologetic. "What I meant was, you can't see the birthmark when she has a shirt on."

"I knew what you meant," Granz answered. "Anything else?"

"Her pink crib blanket is gone, too."

"Did you have Jane finger and footprinted at the hospital when she was born?"

The Alexanders exchanged looks, then he said, "No."

"Have you clipped a lock of her hair?" Mackay asked. "I keep a lock of my daughter's infant hair in a locket."

"No," Gayle answered.

"That's all right, we can obtain hair samples from her hairbrush," Granz told her, then explained that if identity questions arose, her hair could be positively identified through DNA testing.

"Sergeant Miller will obtain fingerprints and hair samples from you, your nanny, and anyone else who visits regularly," he added. "Could you please compile a list of everyone—family, friends, delivery persons, cleaning personnel—who comes and goes routinely from the home."

"Sure."

"Have either of you noticed any prowlers or strangers in the neighborhood or around where you work recently?"

Garrett considered the question. "No."

"Former spouses, creditors, or anyone else who might bear a grudge against either of you?"

"No."

Granz thought for a minute. "Do either of you gamble or use illegal drugs? If so, you must tell us."

Garrett Alexander shook his head. "Good God, what a question!"

Granz waited.

"No. Absolutely not."

"Okay. Just a few more questions," Mackay said. "Does the baby have any health problems?"

"Except for the birthmark, no," Gayle answered.

"She's seen a pediatrician?"

"Yes."

"Routine exams?" Mackay asked.

"And to discuss treatment for the birthmark."

"Treatment?" Granz asked. "I thought port-wine stains were permanent . . ."

Gayle Alexander stared at him before answering. "Defects?"

"I'm sorry. Yes, that's what I meant."

"They are. Laser treatments can help, fade them somewhat, but not until she's a young woman. It's very expensive and the treatments are only marginally effective. Her breast . . . her chest . . . when she gets married, she'll . . ." She didn't need to finish.

Granz nodded. "Do you have any other photos? This one isn't very good, the lighting is poor, and it's out of focus."

Gayle Alexander handed him a second photograph. "We took this right after the bath. They're the only pictures we have of her."

In the second picture, Janey wore a frilly yellow dress, little yellow booties and a yellow bonnet. She stared directly into the camera with her big dark eyes. *She's such a beautiful baby,* Granz thought, and noted that the birthmark was completely covered by the dress.

Granz handed the snapshots to Mackay. She studied them briefly and gave them back to him. He dropped them into his briefcase with the note. "We'll disseminate her picture to local law enforcement agencies. Within a few hours, NCMEC will broadcast fax Jane's picture to every agency in the country."

"What's NCMEC?" Mrs. Alexander asked.

"It stands for the National Center for Missing and Exploited Children, a private clearinghouse for information on missing children. They'll post her picture on their Internet Web site." He slid forward, and started to stand. "Now, my detectives need to gather clothing and bedding from her room so our bloodhounds will have fresh scents to follow. Is that okay?"

"Do you have to put her picture on the Internet?" Gayle asked, her voice rising sharply into a shriek.

Granz settled back into his seat. "It's standard procedure."

Mackay added, "The more publicity we get, the faster we'll find Janey. Can you tell us why you don't want her picture circulated?"

Gayle looked at her husband. "It's the birthmark," he said simply.

"The only picture that'll be posted on the Net is the one in the dress," Mackay assured them. "We'll use the other one only to eliminate false reports, and to confirm her identity when she's located."

"I still don't want her picture broadcast all over the Internet," Gayle protested. "Can't you wait awhile? Maybe you'll find her and it won't be necessary."

"No ma'am, we can't," Granz declared. "The faster we get her picture out, the sooner we'll find her. Now, Detective Miller will be your law enforcement contact," Granz summed up, shutting off any further objections. "He'll assign detectives to monitor incoming telephone calls and arrange to interview your nanny and have her take a polygraph exam."

"A polygraph!"

"It's routine to ask family members and others in the household to take a polygraph so we can eliminate them as suspects immediately and move on to more productive pursuits."

"You want *us* to take lie detector tests?" Gayle asked incredulously.

"As Lieutenant Granz said, it's just routine operating procedure," Mackay explained.

"Absolutely not, lie detectors are notoriously unreliable and unpredictable," Garrett Alexander declared. "We won't do it."

Granz held his hands out, palms down and flat like a baseball umpire making a "safe" signal. "You aren't required to submit to a polygraph examination." He switched off the recorder, and stood up. Mackay followed his cue.

"Thank you very much for your assistance. Please remember that you shouldn't use your phone and if it rings, don't answer it until one of my detectives gives you the go-ahead."

4

"The Alexanders are hiding something, or they'd take a damn poly."

Granz set his briefcase on the floor, indicated for Mackay to sit in one of the ancient Naugahyde chairs in his crowded office, sat behind his desk, and opened the paper coffee cup they had grabbed at the Starbucks cart in the atrium.

Mackay opened her coffee, sipped, and said, "Maybe."

"Maybe my ass! Were you and I at the same interview? Every time I asked a question, they looked at each other and gave me a one-word answer; 'yes' or 'no.' No explanations, no elaboration, and almost no help. A poly'd damn sure tell us why they're so uncooperative."

"Well, polygraph exams are strictly voluntary, so the Alexanders can't be compelled to submit," Mackay countered. "Besides, for most people they're pretty scary, and the Alexanders seem like private people. I don't think they're being uncooperative—I think they're just being cautious. Then there's the birthmark."

He smirked. "You're too gullible. If they weren't hiding something, they'd take it and let us get on with finding their baby."

"I doubt I'd take one, either."

"Bullshit! If someone snatched your kid, you'd submit to a poly in a minute, if you thought it might help get her back."

He drained his coffee, pushed away from the desk, and crossed his legs.

"My detectives'll be conducting two simultaneous investigations: one to eliminate the parents as suspects, the other trying to find the baby and catch the kidnapper. That doesn't make sense from their standpoint, and it damn sure doesn't make sense from mine."

"Polygraphs are only an investigative tool, Dave. You'd look into their backgrounds anyway, no matter what the poly results were."

Granz leaned forward with his elbows on the desk. "Don't lecture me about investigative techniques. I know what polygraphs do. I also know that if they passed, I'd approach the investigation a lot differently."

"I wasn't lecturing."

"Yeah, right! My gut says they aren't leveling with us and I can't overlook the possibility that they're involved."

"I think you're reading them wrong, and overreacting to their reluctance to take a poly," Mackay told him.

"That's why you're the lawyer and I'm the investigator, Kathryn. Eventually, I'll figure out what they're hiding. When I do, I'll turn it over to you, but until then, it's my investigation and I'm gonna follow my instincts."

"You always do," Mackay retorted.

"What the hell does that mean?" he demanded, then added, "If you're referring to my approach to the Gingerbread Man and Lancaster investigations, let me remind you that it was my gut instincts and creative investigative techniques that nailed their asses. If it'd been left to you, we'd still be looking for them."

She shrugged, but refused to accept the bait. "What about publicity? I think you should call a media conference as soon as possible."

"No way," he told her. "What would it accomplish?"

"For one thing, it might expedite the baby's recovery. A sixty-second TV news spot is better than a hundred thousand posters and flyers."

"Yeah, and a hundred thousand times more likely to screw up my investigation."

"How?"

"Phony confessions, crank calls, dead-end leads, false ransom demands. You name it, there's some goddamn nut case out there that'll do it. No thanks."

"Hold back a couple of critical facts, things only the kidnapper would know, to weed out the phonies."

"Thanks for the advice. I'd never have thought of that—I've only done it several hundred times."

Again she ignored his sarcasm. "Just divulge generalities about the note. Withhold the exact contents, the paper color and type, and the fact that it was assembled from cutouts. Also withhold the fact that the baby's blanket was taken. We need some publicity."

"I'll think about it," he agreed.

Mackay glanced at her watch. "I hope so, because if you fail to brief the media, I will."

Granz stood, and Mackay followed. "Don't interfere with my investigation, Kate," he told her.

"Thanks for coffee, Dave," she answered, ignoring his threat. "I'd better get back to my office."

5

Emma Mackay was accustomed to Kathryn's erratic hours, and on nights Kathryn was called out, stayed with their neighbor Ruth, whose liberal phone policy facilitated long, secret conversations with Emma's best friend. At home, strict limits were imposed on telephone use, prompting Emma to accuse her mother of forgetting that by age twelve, a woman must attend to her social as well as her academic obligations.

Kathryn always smiled inwardly at Emma's logic. With a melancholy fondness, she recalled changing from a girl into a young woman, and wanted her daughter to experience the same mystery and wonder. She loved hearing Emma whisper and giggle with her friends about magical things she had almost forgotten. But not at the expense of her studies.

By the time Kathryn left Granz's office, she was late for a Juvenile Justice Task Force meeting. After that meeting concluded, she met with the County

Administrative Officer to discuss the upcoming budget hearings. Then, she stopped by a Chinese food take-out and picked up Emma at Ruth's. By the time they finished dinner, it was almost nine o'clock.

Emma suggested they watch *Ally McBeal* together. When it was over, they were cuddled together on the sofa, and Emma was asleep with her head on her mother's lap. Kathryn brushed Emma's hair from her face.

"Em, it's time to go to bed."

"Are you going to stay up?" Emma yawned.

"For a little while, sweetie. I want to watch the ten o'clock news."

"Can I sleep here with you until the news is over?"

"Sure, I'll wake you when I go to bed."

Kathryn aimed the remote at the TV and scrolled through the channels, stopping when she spotted the stylized Channel 7 News logo fade to the images of co-anchors Steve Wallace and Arliss Kraft.

Arliss tossed out a few teasers, then a color photograph of Jane Alexander appeared in the upper right-hand corner.

"On our six o'clock news this evening," Kraft began, "we reported that a six-week-old baby girl was kidnapped from the bedroom of her Mission Heights home while her parents and nanny slept in nearby rooms. The kidnappers left a note, but law enforcement officials have refused to reveal its contents, or the amount of ransom demanded. Here with an update is Steven Wallace." She smiled and turned. "Steve?"

To Kathryn, Wallace looked like a replica of a

human being, something she would find in a wax museum; perfect in appearance, but totally lifeless. And, in her opinion, he had a personality to match.

"Statistics show that the majority of child abduction cases are perpetrated by the child's parents. Law enforcement normally requires parents to take a lie detector test to establish their innocence before launching a full-scale search. As you will see, that step has not been taken in this kidnapping investigation."

"Just minutes ago," Wallace continued, "I spoke by telephone with Jane Alexander's father. Here is Channel-Seven News' exclusive taped interview with Garrett Alexander."

"Mr Alexander, did the police ask you and your wife to take lie detector tests?"

Garrett Alexander's nervousness manifested itself in a wavering voice. "Yes."

"Have you taken them?"

"No."

"But, you have agreed to do so, haven't you?"

"No."

"Mr. Alexander, our viewers wonder why you and your wife refused to take polygraph examinations unless you have something to hide. Do you have something to hide, sir?"

"No."

"You had nothing to do with your baby's abduction?"

"Absolutely not."

"So, you'll take a lie detector test, then?"

"I won't discuss this further, Mr. Wallace."

"Okay, then tell us what the kidnap note said."

"I've been told to not discuss it with the media."

"Who told you not to talk to us?"

"The District Attorney."

"I see. How much money have the kidnappers demanded for the return of your daughter?"

"I'm not supposed to say," Alexander told him. "I agreed to this interview only because of your implied threat to accuse my wife and me of somehow being involved in our daughter's abduction if we didn't deny it publicly. Well, we do deny it categorically."

"So, you refuse to continue the interview?"

"I've done everything I agreed to."

The tape clicked off and the screen faded to a head and shoulder shot of Wallace and Kraft.

"As you can see, there are many unanswered questions surrounding the mysterious disappearance of Jane Alexander. Now, back to you, Arliss, for the rest of the news."

"Mom, who stole those people's baby?" Emma asked.

"I thought you were asleep. Did you hear?"

"Yeah. Who did it?"

"We don't know yet."

"Do you think they'll pay the kidnappers to get their baby back?"

"Of course they will, if that's what it takes."

Emma sat up. "Would you pay if someone kidnaped me?"

"Of course I would."

"What if you couldn't get enough money?"

"Why are you asking me all these questions? Did the story scare you?"

"Maybe a little," she replied, then added, "But no one would ever take me, Mom."

"I know, because we're very careful."

"Even if they did, they'd bring me home in a few hours."

"Oh really? Why?"

"Because I'm almost thirteen years old, and no one could put up with a teenager for very long."

6

"That's deep enough. The goddam hole doesn't have to go all the way to China."

She stepped out onto high ground and threw the folding military shovel at his head, but missed. "If you don't like the way I do it, dig the hole yourself."

He flicked the butt of his Marlboro into the hole and lit another, then leaned against the trunk of a fledgling redwood tree and crossed his arms over his chest, cigarette dangling from his lips.

"Ask me, we shoulda just tossed the fucker in the Dumpster behind Safeway."

The glowing tip of his cigarette bobbed up and down when he spoke, which just made her angrier. Tears ran down her cheeks.

"Go to hell," she said.

He stood upright and walked toward his partner until his face was inches from hers. "I've put up with your bleeding-heart crap long enough, bitch," he spat. "Now, toss the damn thing in and cover it up with dirt before I kick your ass into the hole behind him and cover you both up with dirt."

Cigarette ashes fell on her chest, and his tobacco-alcohol breath made her sick to her stomach. She turned and threw up into the hole, then wiped her eyes and chin on the sleeve of her jacket. "Fuck!"

He laughed, chucked the second Marlboro butt into the hole, and lit one more with a paper match, which he threw in behind the butt. He checked the pack and discovered it was empty, cursed, wadded it up and tossed it in, as well. Then with the toe of his Tony Lama boot, he kicked an oblong object into the hole behind the trash. It was wrapped in a motel blanket, and hit bottom with a mushy thump.

"Cover it up," he ordered, handing her the shovel.

She refused to accept it. "Cover it up yourself, you sonofabitch." She shivered and drew her jacket tight around her. "This was your stupid idea. I'll wait for you at the car."

Five minutes later, he crawled behind the steering wheel and tossed the shovel into the backseat. "I missed the end of the movie," he said, "and Bogart's my favorite. Damn good thing for you I'm an understanding guy."

"Fuck you," she snarled.

He laughed, then coughed, spit the phlegm out the window, and pulled a fresh pack of Marlboros from over the sun visor. He lit one with the lighter, replaced the still-glowing lighter in the dashboard, then started the engine.

He was still coughing and laughing when they drove away from the park entrance with the headlights off.

7

SANTA RITA COUNTY
DISTRICT ATTORNEY'S OFFICE
WEDNESDAY, 8:15 A.M.

Kathryn Mackay parked in the area reserved for elected officials, department heads, and VIPs.

The squat, square, five-story Santa Rita, California County Government Center building was constructed at the height of the Cold War from rebar and unpainted concrete. Inside, stone-floored corridors, cold fluorescent lights, and gray metal walls furnished a functional place to work, but no more. The only color was an occasional art exhibit by local talent, which few county employees noticed.

Mackay walked briskly upstairs, where a receptionist ensconced behind bulletproof glass buzzed her through an electronically controlled security door.

District Attorneys' offices filled most of the second floor, beneath the Sheriff's Department, which occupied the entire third level, an arrangement which at times facilitated communications between the county's primary law enforcement agency and its prosecutors.

Hallways divided the DAs' space into quadrants, with concrete pillars spaced at twenty-five foot intervals supporting the ceiling. HVAC ducts and conduit hung from the overhead, which was sprayed with soundproofing that was ineffectual at eliminating noise from the Sheriff's Department above.

Metal panels bolted to the floor and ceiling chopped the interior into a labyrinth of offices, conference rooms, law library, a coffee room, and work stations. One hallway stopped at District Attorney Mackay's office door, which was flanked by those of her Chief Deputy and Chief of Inspectors.

Mackay closed the door behind her, and settled into the high-backed desk chair. Years earlier as an Assistant DA, Mackay's office made a statement. Tossing out the government-issue furniture, she spent her own money on an executive desk and leather interview chairs. One by one, she accumulated headlines and news articles from dozens of her spectacular courtroom victories, had them professionally matted and framed, and hung them on the walls of her office.

They were not a show of ego, but intended to instill confidence in witnesses and victims of violent crimes; confidence that *someone* in the system advocated for them and their families; confidence that, despite the misnomer applied to court-appointed defense lawyers, it was *she* who was the "Public Defender."

Unrelenting criticism by a defense lawyer, however, eventually drove her to relocate the display to her small home office, where only she and Emma saw it. After she won her first reelection as DA by a landslide, she restored the clippings to their rightful place in her office.

At nine-thirty, she walked to the atrium that separated county administrative offices from the courts building, and bought a small coffee from the Starbucks cart. When she returned to her office, she picked up her desk phone.

A faint, hollow echo was discernible on the line when Gayle Alexander answered.

"Mrs. Alexander, this is District Attorney Mackay."

"Yes?"

"Since we've heard nothing from the kidnappers, we need to call a media conference."

"We don't want you to do that, Ms. Mackay."

"You have no choice."

The line was silent for several seconds. "Neither my husband nor I will attend."

"I don't understand, Mrs. Alexander. Why would you refuse to attend if it might help us find your baby and return her to you?"

"We have our reasons."

"We need to publicize Jane's abduction," Mackay insisted. "No matter how careful the kidnappers are, they can't entirely avoid public exposure. Media coverage is the best way to generate leads from the public, because the media can get her story and picture in front of a large number of people, one of whom might know something that could help us locate Janey quickly. Time is not on her side."

"We are considering offering a reward."

Mackay contemplated. "In my opinion, an immediate media briefing is our best hope. Rewards are occasionally helpful, but normally they're less useful immediately following the abduction than after a period of time has elapsed. But, if you feel strongly about it, I suggest that you and your husband contact your family attorney. Reward offers raise complex legal issues. Do you have an attorney?"

"Yes, she's in San Jose."

"Contact her first thing tomorrow morning. She can advise you on the legal issues, then handle the details if you still believe a reward is appropriate."

"We will."

"Now, about the media conference," Mackay persisted. "I can brief the reporters, but it's crucial that either you or your husband, or both of you, are with me so TV viewers can see you and relate to your tragedy. The media will ask questions they want one of you to answer personally. I have a good idea what questions they'll ask and can help you prepare, but you'll have to speak at some point. Do you have a fax machine at home?"

"Yes."

"I'll fax an explanatory pamphlet on conducting media interviews and turning the media into your allies in the search for your child," Mackay explained. "After you've read it, we'll prepare a package for each media representative; photos, a description of Jane and the clothing she was wearing, a description of where and how she was taken, and a phone number for people to call with leads."

"I thought you wanted us to keep all the home phone lines clear."

"We do. It's a special line into the DA's office with

tracing, trapping and recording equipment already installed. It was set up precisely for this purpose, and will be monitored by one of my inspectors. I'll announce the number during the press conference."

"Where will it be held?"

"The Board of Supervisors chambers. Will you try to make it?"

"I don't think so, but I'll discuss it with Garrett."

Mackay sighed but exhibited no other signs of the exasperation and frustration she felt boiling up inside.

"I'll have my secretary start contacting the media immediately, to set up a briefing for three o'clock. I'll leave my office at five minutes before three to walk upstairs. If you aren't here by then, I'll conduct the briefing by myself."

"I understand."

I doubt it, Mackay thought. *You couldn't possibly understand how bad this makes you look, even to me. If you did, you'd be there. And, you'd take a polygraph.*

She said, "I hope so. This may be the best chance we have to recover Janey, and if you don't make the most of it, you might never see her again."

"I know."

8

"Dammit!"

Kathryn Mackay checked her watch and grabbed a manila folder from her desk. Hoping that the Alexanders would relent at the last minute, she waited until 3:15, and was now late for the media conference.

The Fire Marshal posted the Board of Supervisors chambers for 170 persons, and it was packed, reporters in half the seats, law enforcement personnel from local and neighboring jurisdictions, curious spectators, and a few homeless occupying the remainder. Camera operators and their tripod-mounted equipment lined the side and rear walls, and the floor in front of the raised dais.

As soon as the District Attorney entered the room and strode down the center aisle, the crowd fell almost silent, and the room emitted only the ubiquitous murmur unique to spaces packed with expectant, excited people.

Mackay sat in the chairperson's spot at the center of the dais and squinted into the media lights.

"At approximately three o'clock yesterday morning, unknown persons forcibly entered a Mission Heights home and kidnapped a six-week-old infant girl while she slept," she stated without preamble. "Her name is Jane Alexander.

"Law enforcement has mobilized every resource at its disposal, including scent-tracking bloodhounds and aircraft equipped with heat-detecting and infrared devices capable of locating an infant on the ground even in dense foliage or inside small buildings.

"Today, I ask for your assistance in helping us to return Jane Alexander to her parents quickly and safely, and to apprehend the kidnappers. As you leave, you will each receive a packet that contains a description of Jane and the clothing she was wearing, as well as Jane's photograph. It also includes details about the crime as we know them at this early stage of the investigation.

"Finally, the packet contains a telephone number set up as a public hot line for tips and information. We implore anyone with information, no matter how insignificant it may seem, to call that number, anonymously if they wish, to report it. Please give the hot-line number extensive publicity."

A dozen hands shot up from reporters, but Mackay said, "Please allow me to finish, then I'll answer your questions."

She stared into the nearest light bank. "This is a recent photograph of Jane Alexander," she said, holding the baby's picture up for the camera. "If you see this infant, or think you know her whereabouts, please call the number that I've provided previously."

Mackay sipped from a glass of ice water. "Thank you for your patience. I'll accept your questions now."

"Why aren't the parents here?" a reporter shouted.

"As you can imagine, they are overwrought at the loss of their daughter," Mackay hedged.

"Are the parents suspects?" another reporter asked. Mackay recognized the voice.

"Everyone is a suspect until we establish otherwise, Mr. Wallace. In an investigation of this nature, the early stages focus on eliminating as many people as possible, so we can pursue legitimate leads. Law enforcement hasn't had time to conclusively eliminate anyone as a suspect, including the parents, but we have no reason to believe that either Garrett or Gayle Alexander had anything to do with their baby's abduction."

"Was anyone besides the baby at home when she was kidnapped?" Wallace followed up.

"Mr. and Mrs. Alexander were asleep in their bedroom. Jane's nanny was asleep in a bedroom adjoining the nursery."

"Ms. Mackay, you used the term 'perpetrators,' plural," a female reporter asked. "Were there more than one kidnapper?"

Mackay contemplated her response. "Certain evidence at the scene suggests there were more than one, but we won't know for sure until all the evidence has been examined."

Holding a microphone toward the dais, the MBTV news anchor from Monterey asked, "How did the kidnappers get into the house?"

"They forced the second story window of Jane's room."

"How?"

"I can't discuss those details."

"Was there an alarm system?" another reporter inquired.

"Yes. The perpetrators successfully disabled it."

"How?"

"I can't share that information with you at this time."

"Has the FBI been called in?" Steve Wallace asked.

"We will be in touch with them today," Mackay responded. "Technically, Federal authorities have no jurisdiction unless the victim is transported across state lines, and we have no reason to believe that's the case. But Federal law provides that if the victim isn't recovered within twenty-four hours, she is presumed to have been taken out of state. This permits the FBI to respond if the local jurisdiction requests assistance."

"You're referring to the Lindbergh Law?"

"That's what it's commonly called, yes."

Mackay unconsciously clenched her fists, then willed herself to relax, knowing she would hear from Dave Granz as soon as the interview was concluded.

"Did the kidnappers leave a note behind?" a newspaper reporter asked.

"Yes," Mackay responded.

"How much money did the ransom note demand?"

"I didn't say it was a ransom note," Mackay replied quickly.

"Then, what did it say?" the same woman wanted to know.

Mackay knew she walked a thin line between divulging too much, and alienating the very reporters whose cooperation might be pivotal to Jane Alexander's return. "I can't comment further on the note."

A reporter in the second row stood. "What are the chances of recovering the baby alive? I understand that far fewer victims are found alive than not."

Mackay clasped her hands and leaned forward on her elbows. "We'll find her alive, sir. Now, if there are no more questions—"

"Just one more."

Steve Wallace stood, as had Mackay, preparing to leave. "Can the police require the parents to take lie detector tests?"

"No," Mackay answered.

"Too bad," he commented.

"That's what I was thinking," she mumbled to herself as she headed for the stairs.

9

"Sonofabitch!" Granz slung his half-full coffee cup into the garbage can next to the Starbucks cart in the atrium. The portable radio on which he had listened to the media conference tumbled in behind it and plopped into a congealed mass of cold cappuccino and soggy, half-eaten muffins.

He reached to the bottom of the can, then reconsidered and dropped the dripping radio back into the abyss. "Motherfucker," he said, and kicked the can over onto its side.

"Sir?" the coffee attendant said tentatively.

Granz glanced at her apologetically, mumbled "Sorry," righted the garbage can, and headed for Mackay's office. He almost bowled her over when he barged onto the second floor landing of the stairwell.

Hollow echoes shot upward, ricocheted down from the ceiling, rebounded off the basement floor, and reverberated through the concrete and steel stairwell. It reeked of fresh paint, mildew and Lysol, but neither of them noticed anymore; it had become part of everyday life.

"What was that crap about calling in the FBI?" he demanded. "You had no right to say we should ask for help. It's a Sheriff's Office investigation, and I'll decide if I need help from the feds."

Mackay stopped and turned. "Good afternoon to you, too, Lieutenant. I was asked my opinion, and I gave it. If you hadn't chosen to skip the media conference, they would have asked you that question, and you could have answered for yourself."

"Dammit, Kathryn—"

She resumed walking, and he followed. "Why don't we discuss this back in my office," Mackay suggested.

When they settled into the leather chairs, Granz said, "Let's declare a truce, Kate."

She stared at him. "I'm willing, but I'm not the one who jumped your case at the Alexander crime scene."

"I guess you're right. But that was then, this is now. I'll try to lighten up if you will."

Mackay thought it over. "Either leave your personal feelings about me at home in the morning, Dave, or assign one of your detectives to work with me on this. It's too hard being at each other's throats," she told him.

"Agreed." He crossed his legs. "What now? The press isn't going to back off their position that the Alexanders are involved until they submit to polys. Do you think they will, after that briefing?"

"Maybe." Mackay pursed her lips. "Let's find out."

She punched the speaker button on her desk phone and dialed. When Gayle Alexander answered, Mackay said, "This is DA Mackay, Mrs. Alexander. Lieutenant Granz is with me and I have you on speaker phone. Did you and Mr. Alexander see the media conference?"

"We watched it. I don't understand why the reporters think we're responsible for Janey's disappearance."

"You can't blame them," Granz countered. "That's one reason we ask parents to take a polygraph, to squelch the skepticism. Think about the Jon-Benet Ramsey murder in Colorado. Didn't you wonder why the parents refused to take a polygraph?"

"I suppose so," she conceded.

"Then, will you take a polygraph exam now, Mrs. Alexander?"

"What if we say no?" she asked.

"Then it'll take longer for Lieutenant Granz's detectives to establish your innocence, time they could spend looking for Jane," Mackay explained.

"How does it work?"

"Well, it's basically pretty simple," Granz explained. "A polygraph is really several instruments combined to simultaneously record changes in certain of the body's autonomic functions; blood pressure, pulse and respiration rates, and the skin's resistance to an electrical current. Those functions change when a person lies, and they're almost impossible to control consciously."

"How are the changes recorded?"

"The examiner attaches a pneumograph tube around your chest, several small electrodes on your fingers and hands, and an ordinary blood-pressure cuff on one arm. The readings picked up by these sensors are synchronized through a small portable panel unit and transmitted as parallel lines on moving graph paper. The graphs are then interpreted by the examiner to determine if your responses are truthful."

"How does the examiner know what my normal readings are?"

"You provide some simple information to the examiner, who asks you about them and records your responses to establish a baseline against which he can measure and interpret your responses to other questions."

"What kind of information?"

"Things that are straightforward, nonstressful, and easy to answer; your name, address, where you work, your husband's name, your age, the date you gave birth to your baby, for example."

The line went silent. "Mrs. Alexander, are you still there?" Mackay asked.

"Yes, we're both here, Ms. Mackay. I'm sorry, but neither Garrett nor I are willing to take a lie detector test."

Mackay sighed, and looked at Granz, who was shaking his head as if to say, "I told you they were guilty."

"I really think you should reconsider," Mackay told them. "The examiner could be at your home within an hour, and it would be over by this evening."

"We've made our decision," Garrett Alexander interjected.

* * *

Kathryn was approaching the parking lot when her pager beeped. Although she didn't recognize the number, it was followed by 9-1-1, a technique sometimes employed by law enforcement, and her daughter, Emma, to indicate that the call was urgent.

She immediately pulled a cell phone from her handbag and punched in the page number.

A man's muffled voice answered.

"Yes?"

"This is Kathryn Mackay."

"I know. Be quiet and listen, I won't repeat myself. I have Jane Alexander."

"How do I know you have her?"

"The ransom note was made of letters and words cut from newspapers."

"So are half the notes in a thousand kidnappings every year," Mackay answered softly, carefully negotiating the tightrope between antagonizing him into hanging up, and not being sure she was talking to the real kidnapper.

"Give me something more to work with," she asked.

"If you keep fucking with me, Mackay, I'll hang up and no one will ever see the kid again."

"Don't hang up," Mackay said. "I need to be sure, that's all."

He paused a few seconds, then said, "The ladder was yellow fiberglass. The alarm system was disabled with a couple of safety pins and alligator clips."

She looked around, saw no one, and leaned against her car. "How did you get my pager number?"

"I told your secretary I snatched the kid."

"We get a lot of crank calls. She believed you?"

"No, but I told her that her ass'd be grass if she guessed wrong, and didn't give me your number."

"Why call me?"

"Because the parents' phone is monitored, but your cell phone probably isn't, and digital cell transmissions are almost impossible to trace. Now, tell the Alexanders to assemble two million dollars in fives, tens, and twenties, nothing bigger. And no new bills, no dye, no dust, and no exploding stain bombs or consecutive serial numbers. If you mark the bills in any way, I'll kill the kid."

"How do the Alexanders notify you when they've got the money?" she asked.

"It's 5:45 P.M. In forty-eight hours, your pager will go off. Be with the parents when it does. I'll tell them where to take the money. If there ain't any fuckups with the cash drop—and I mean *No* fuckups—I'll call back and tell you where to find the kid."

"Anything else?"

"Yes, and listen up, Mackay, because the kid's life is in *your* hands. Don't play games or let anything go wrong. If the slightest thing looks suspicious, or you don't follow instructions exactly, you'll be killing that kid just as sure as if you pulled the trigger. Do I make myself clear?"

"Yes, but I—" she started to protest, but the line was already dead.

10

FOGBANK INN
THURSDAY, 4:05 A.M.

"Yeah," he said into the bedside phone.

"It's me," she told him.

"What do you want? I'm watchin' Casablanca."

"Don't you ever sleep?"

"Not if I can help it. What do you care?"

She shook her head and covered the phone with her hand. "Sonofabitch," she whispered. Then into the phone said, "Turn the television down so we can talk."

He fluffed up the pillow, leaned back, and drew deep on his Marlboro.

"Talk. I can hear you."

"You idiot, this is serious. Turn the damn TV down."

He sighed and muted the TV sound, but never removed his eyes from the screen. "All right, go," he told her.

She moved some papers out of her way and leaned on her elbows, holding the phone to her left ear. "She started about an hour ago and is well along."

"How much longer?"

"Barring complications, an hour, more or less."

"The movie's not over till five-thirty," he said, then coughed deep in his chest but didn't cover the mouthpiece. Then he warned, "You make damned sure there ain't any complications."

"She's someone else's responsibility, but I've offered to help. As soon as she finishes, I'll beep your walkie-talkie three times, then medicate her. It acts quick, so when I beep, get here fast. If you're not here when I'm ready, we'll miss the opportunity."

"I'll do my job. Make sure you do yours, and do it right this time."

"I know how to do my job."

"Yeah, that's why we had to toss the last reject in the trash, 'cause you're so good at your job. This time make sure it ain't defective, or we'll hafta take another drive to the park, and you didn't like it there."

"You sonofabitch," she said, then hung up.

5:45 A.M.

"It took you long enough to get here," she complained.

"I watched the end of the movie," he said, the glowing tip of the Marlboro bobbing up and down. "Give me the damn thing so I can get outta here, these places give me the creeps."

"Put the cigarette out, you're dropping ashes all over the place."

He flipped the smoke to the ground and smashed it with the toe of his boot. "All right, now give it to me."

She handed down a wrapped bundle, which he inspected, then dropped casually on the passenger seat of the car.

"Be careful, dammit, the way I showed you," she admonished him.

"Don't worry about it. Just get back to the room as soon as you can. I don't like these things."

"I get off at six. I'll be there by quarter after. And everything had better be all right when I get there this time."

He lit a Marlboro, dragged deeply, then coughed and spat on the driveway. "Or what?"

11

SANTA RITA COUNTY EASTSIDE
THURSDAY, 6:15 A.M.

Except for a wheelchair ramp beside the front steps, and lights blazing inside, 243 Via del Robles looked like every other house in the old neighborhood. A silver Toyota Corolla, headlights on high beam, careened around the corner and screeched to a halt in the narrow driveway. The driver's door slammed open and a tall woman in her early fifties, wearing a sweatshirt, Levis and open-heel Birkenstocks, spilled out and dashed toward the front steps, long gray hair trailing behind.

Halfway across the lawn, she stumbled over a low, carved wooden sign mounted on discreet redwood posts:

REDWOOD ALTERNATIVE HEALTH CARE—PREGNANCY
COUNSELING AND BIRTHING CENTER.

Unfazed, she charged up the concrete stairs and twisted the front doorknob, but it was locked. Fumbling through her handbag failed to produce a key, so she leaned on the doorbell.

A large woman wearing a name tag that read, GRETCHEN POTTER, MIDWIFE, pinned to blue scrubs, peeked through the crack, recognized her boss, and swung the door open. "Eve, I'm so glad you're here. I can't believe it, I just can't believe it. I just—"

Evelyn Franchette grasped the woman's arm and guided her to a sofa in the waiting area. "Calm down, Gretchen, and tell me what happened."

"The Sweet baby is gone."

"Are you sure his mother doesn't have him?"

"Of course I'm sure, I looked in on her first. Karen's asleep and the baby isn't there."

"You checked the other two birthing rooms?"

"Yes, and the bathrooms. He's not there, either."

"He's got to be. Let's check the nursery again," Evelyn ordered.

They walked briskly down a hallway, past three doors marked BIRTHING ROOM. One was closed with a handwritten nameplate inserted into a brass holder: *Karen Sweet*. The remaining doors were open, the rooms vacant.

The nursery occupied an entire rear corner of the building, and contained three cribs. Potter stopped beside one. "This is where he was."

Evelyn stood for a moment, squeezing her lower lip in contemplation. "Okay, I'll recheck inside, maybe you overlooked something. He's here someplace." As an afterthought, she added, "He's got to be."

Evelyn searched the two vacant rooms and bathrooms, dropping to her hands and knees to peer under the metal framed beds with a flashlight. Bypassing the occupied room, she slid all the furniture from the waiting and reception areas to the center of the room and overturned them. She lifted and checked under each area rug, and emptied the storage rooms. Finding nothing, she replaced the furniture and repeated the process in the office.

By the time she returned to the nursery, tears of frustration ran down her cheeks. She opened every cabinet to check inside, and searched the walk-in storage room, where nursery supplies were kept. As a last resort, she opened the refrigerator.

"Damn!" she screamed, and slammed the refrigerator door. It sprang open and she slammed it again, then sat at a small table, leaned on her elbows, head in hands, and began to sob.

Gretchen returned and sat beside her boss, her hand on Evelyn Franchette's shoulder.

"What do we do now, Evie?"

"We can't wait any longer. I'll call the police."

12

Lieutenant Dave Granz parked behind Sergeant Jazzbo Miller's green Volkswagen Passat. Yellow crime scene tape was strung around the perimeter of the small lot, and uniformed deputies guarded each corner.

Miller stood talking to a female detective in the driveway, toward the rear of the house in front of a detached one-car garage. They were looking at the side of the house when Miller spotted his boss, said something to the detective, and walked to Granz' Explorer.

He slid into the passenger seat. "Damn, that heater feels good," he said, and handed a plastic evidence bag to Granz. "Cigarette. Doesn't belong to anyone in the house; they don't allow smoking anywhere on the premises. Looks like the perp dropped it. If we ever get a suspect, we can submit it for DNA testing to match it to the suspect's saliva."

"Show me where you found it," Granz said, inspecting the smashed Marlboro butt.

They ducked under the crime scene tape, and Miller led Granz down a narrow driveway with concrete wheel strips separated by grass, along the west side of the house. "No shoe tracks, everything's cement," he commented, pointing to where the driveway abutted the structure's foundation.

"Tire tracks?"

"Nada. Can't even say for sure that whoever it was drove a car, but I'm sure they did."

"Prob'ly, anybody walking through the neighborhood before dawn would attract unwelcome attention."

Miller grunted agreement. "I think someone brought the kid through here." He indicated an old-fashioned wood casement window at the rear corner of the house. The bottom was fully raised, and there was no screen.

"It was open when we got here."

Granz shined his flashlight across the sill at an oblique angle, and leaned over to inspect it. "The dust has been disturbed recently."

"Yeah, Yamamoto and his CSI unit's on the way," Miller told him.

"Who called nine-one-one?"

Miller looked in his notebook. "Evelyn Franchette. Deputies responded, searched inside the house, then secured the scene. Detectives are going door-to-door now, interviewing neighbors."

"Where's Franchette?"

"Inside. She owns the business."

"Business? Isn't this a private residence?"

"Nope, it's a clinic where women have babies."

"Here? Why the hell don't they go to a hospital?" Granz asked.

Miller shrugged. "Got me. Let's go talk to Franchette."

The wide concrete front porch was painted a shiny, immaculate, battleship gray. Evelyn Franchette answered the door before they could ring the bell. Her long gray hair was disheveled and her eyes were puffy and red. Granz and Miller showed their identification, and passed her business cards, which she accepted with trembling hands.

"This way, please," she told them.

The living room had been divided into a waiting area, and a reception cubicle that functioned as the office. Franchette sat in an overstuffed chair, and motioned Granz and Miller to a sofa.

She interwove her fingers, clenched her hands and placed them in her lap, and rested her elbows on the chair arms. "Nothing like this has ever happened before," she said.

"Yes, ma'am," Miller answered. "Can you tell us exactly what you do here?"

Franchette handed a business card to each officer. "I own the house and the business. I'm a Certified Nurse Midwife; a registered nurse with a master's degree in midwifery."

"You delivered the baby that's missing?"

"No, I employ another midwife, Gretchen Potter. She attended the birth of the Sweet infant at about five o'clock this morning."

"Where is Gretchen now?"

"With Karen Sweet." Franchette swallowed hard. "Newborns usually stay with their mothers the entire time they're here, but after Karen gave birth, she felt sick, so Gretchen moved her baby into the nursery."

"Show us the nursery," Granz directed.

"Is that window usually open?" Miller asked.

She looked puzzled. "No, we usually keep it closed. Sometimes we open it to get fresh air, this old house doesn't have very good circulation. But it's so cold this morning, it should be shut."

"You didn't ask who opened it when you got here?"

"I guess I was so upset I didn't notice. Probably one of the midwives."

"Except for Mrs. Sweet and Potter, who else was here when the baby disappeared?" Miller asked.

"Karen Sweet isn't married," Franchette corrected him. "No one. The midwife who assisted with the birth had already gone home, and—"

"A second midwife?"

"Two midwives attend each birth. When I'm not available, I hire a temp through an agency."

"The temp's name?" Granz asked.

"Monica Fraley."

Granz nodded his head and flicked a thumb toward the birthing room. Miller disappeared into the room where Karen Sweet and Gretchen Potter were, and returned after two or three minutes.

"Neither of them opened that window," he told Granz.

"Ms. Franchette, would you get me the name of

the temp agency?" Granz asked, and followed her into the office, where she jotted the agency's name and phone number on a slip of paper. "MedTemps, in San Jose," she said, "but . . ."

"But what?"

Franchette cleared her throat. "Is there any way this could be handled, shall we say . . . discreetly? Hold off contacting the placement agency until the baby is found? I would be very grateful."

Granz didn't respond, so she continued. " Rumors of missing babies would be devastating to prospective parents, Lieutenant, especially those who plan nontraditional births. Not to mention it would ruin my clinic."

Granz shut off the tape recorder. "Rumors of missing babies and your business reputation will be the least of our problems if we don't find that baby in the next few minutes."

"What does that mean?"

"As soon as the media broadcasts this story, hundreds of kooks will call us claiming to be, or to know, the kidnapper. We'll have to check every tip, and our investigation'll slow to a crawl. But we can't withhold this from the media—it's against department policy. Besides, they already know."

"They do? How?"

"Scanners. Reporters and news editors listen to emergency dispatch radio transmissions. Every radio and TV station for a hundred miles is already gearing up to make this the lead story on its next newscast."

"Emergency dispatch?"

"Nine-one-one. You called them."

Franchette rose and walked to the door. "Media coverage could cause irreparable damage, Lieutenant."

"Tell me about it," he muttered.

13

"All rise," the bailiff ordered. "Superior Court of the State of California, County of Santa Rita, is now in session, the Honorable Judge Jemima Tucker, presiding."

Jemima Tucker was a beautiful black woman with a quick wit and a quicker temper, who tolerated no nonsense in her courtroom, and when she swept into the room trailing her long black robe, everyone fell silent.

Dave Granz slipped quietly into a front row seat on the left side of the spectator gallery, behind a low oak barrier. Kathryn Mackay sat just inside the railing, a thick manila folder on the prosecutors' table in front of her, flanked on each side by an assistant DA.

Orange-jumpsuited jail inmates filled most of the jury box to the judge's right. A few defense attorneys sat in the custody box with their clients, while three others occupied the chairs at the defense counsel table waiting for the court to call their clients' cases.

When Tucker had settled into her chair behind the bench, the bailiff ordered, "Be seated."

"The Court notes that District Attorney Mackay is present in court this morning," Tucker said, facing the prosecution table. "On what matter are you appearing, Ms. Mackay?"

Mackay stood. "The Berroa habeas, Your Honor."

"I imagine the District Attorney has other things to do this morning. I'll call the Berroa matter first." Tucker sifted through a bucket that held the files for that morning's calendar in the order they were to be heard, located a thick stack of files, and placed them on the bench.

Tucker indicated to the court reporter that transcription should commence, then said, "The record shall reflect that District Attorney Kathryn Mackay is present representing the People and that petitioner Eduardo Berroa, who is not present, is proceeding in pro per."

Berroa was a doctor with a penchant for sexually molesting his young, female Hispanic patients. In exchange for Mackay's dismissing sexual assault charges, Berroa testified against Dr. Robert Simmons, County Health Officer, for the murder of Mackay's predecessor, District Attorney Harold Benton. In addition, Simmons had involved himself in a romantic relationship with Mackay to try to avoid detection and, when that failed, he tried to kill her as well. And almost succeeded.

Mackay charged and convicted Berroa of the involuntary manslaughter of one of his Hispanic patients, who died from a botched abortion he performed, but Simmons had eluded law enforcement and Mackay by fleeing the country.

"Petitioner alleges that he was denied his constitutional right to a fair trial, due to the prosecution's suppression of substantial material evidence of such significance that it would have affected the outcome of the trial," Tucker read from the motion.

"Petitioner further alleges that false evidence, which was substantially material and probative on the issue of guilt, was introduced against him at trial and—"

"Judge, this is a frivolous and fraudulent attempt on Berroa's part to get out from under his four-year prison sentence."

"Finally," Tucker continued, ignoring the interruption, "Petitioner alleges that he was denied his right to a pre-sentencing probation report that might have mitigated the severity of his sentence."

Tucker paused and flipped through the file, removed her reading glasses and leaned forward on the bench with her elbows. "He's right about the probation report."

"He waived the probation report."

Tucker looked up. "The defendant has every right to bring this habeas, Ms. Mackay. Of course, he also has the burden of proving all the facts upon which he relies to overturn the conviction. The District Attorney is directed to file an answer no later than one week from today. The District Attorney shall also cause a copy of her answer to be served on Petitioner at the Soledad Correctional Facility."

Mackay picked up the file. Granz held the low swinging gate for her and said softly, "I need to talk to you."

14

SANTA RITA
UNIVERSITY HEIGHTS
THURSDAY, 8:45 A.M.

"It's too soon. And we can't just leave the baby in the motel room alone. What if something happens to him?"

"Somethin' already happened to him, you dumb broad. What's he gonna do, go out for pizza and beer? And how long you think it'll be till the cops figure it out, and wrap up every birthing place for fifty miles, tight as a drum? We're gonna grab a couple more kids today, or you ain't gettin' paid for any of 'em."

"Damn you, I'd better get paid, or I'll quit."

His answer was slow and deliberate, and each word was enunciated precisely. "You listen to me, and you listen carefully. You get paid for snatching babies, and you get paid very well. If you even think about backing out of the deal you made, you won't live long enough to spend twenty-five cents, much less twenty-five thousand dollars. And that assumes you got paid, which you wouldn't. No one quits. You got that?"

"I can't just walk into a birthing center unannounced without an agency referral. I'll never get near a baby."

"Sure you will, you've got on your nurse outfit. Just waltz in like you own the place, tell 'em the agency sent you over, that they was supposed to call and there must be a mixup, and grab a kid while they ain't watching."

"We don't even know there'll be a newborn at the next one."

"Goddammit!" He flicked the Marlboro butt in her direction, but it bounced off the passenger window and landed on the floorboard. She rolled the window down and dropped it outside the car. He lit another and stuck it into his mouth.

"If there ain't a kid at this one, we'll try the next one, and the next, until we do find one. Read me the address of the next place."

She checked a typewritten list. "Three-oh-seven High Street."

15

Granz dropped into one of Mackay's leather chairs at quarter past three. The other was occupied by DA Inspector Escalante.

Donna Escalante was in her early thirties but looked younger. Tall, slender, and athletic, she moved and held herself with a catlike grace that compelled a second look. Short, straight, jet black hair accentuated strong Mayan features which, devoid of makeup except for faint lipstick, weren't exactly pretty, but attractive in a scrubbed, wholesome way.

She had worked with Granz on several occasions and quickly earned his professional respect. DA Chief Inspector James Fields once described her to Granz as a savvy cop whose instincts were better than most detectives' with twenty years on the job. Granz was convinced after their first investigation together and routinely requested that she work with him.

"Good afternoon, Lieutenant," Escalante greeted him when he sat down.

Granz had told her to call him by his first name but actually appreciated her professional demeanor, which he returned in kind. "Hello, Inspector."

"Inspector Escalante," Mackay said, "Lieutenant Granz has asked for our help, and I've assigned you to assist his investigation as long as you're needed." She turned to Granz. "Lieutenant, will you bring us up to speed?"

"You've filled Escalante in on the kidnapping from the Redwood birthing center this morning?"

"As much as I know based on what you told me earlier."

Granz nodded. "At about ten o'clock this morning, someone snatched another newborn, this one from the University Birthing Center on High Street. A Caucasian male infant."

"MO?" Mackay asked.

"Same perps. Someone inside slid him through an open window to an accomplice outside, shortly after he was born."

Escalante jotted something on a yellow legal pad, and asked, "You're sure it's the same kidnappers?"

Granz nodded. "No, but investigators found a Marlboro butt on the ground outside the window. We took it to DOJ for comparison to the other one, but I suspect it was left there by the same guy that dropped one when they grabbed the Sweet baby."

"Guy?" Escalante queried.

"Marlboros are a middle-aged guy's cigarette. They're not the smoke of choice for younger men, and certainly not for women."

Before Mackay could react, Escalante replied, "I

used to smoke Marlboros myself, Lieutenant. Maybe we shouldn't jump to sexist conclusions."

Granz looked first at Mackay, who shrugged, then at Escalante, who returned his gaze without flinching. "You're right, Inspector. I apologize."

"I just don't want to overlook any possibilities, Lieutenant," Escalante told him. "Now, have I got this right? Somebody drives up to a house in a respectable residential neighborhood in broad daylight, grabs a newborn baby through a window from an accomplice on the inside, then drives away, and no one saw anything?"

"That's about it," Granz conceded. "The side of the house where the baby was removed faces an alley and is invisible except to the adjacent neighbors. No one was home there, my guess is they were at work like everyone else in the neighborhood. CSI took plaster casts of some tire tracks in the alley, but the alley's dirt covered with forty years of gravel overlays. I doubt they'll tell us much."

"I called Women's Health Services," Granz continued. "There are about a dozen private birthing centers scattered around the county, all in small converted single family houses, mostly in older neighborhoods."

"That raises a pretty frightening possibility," Mackay interjected. "We've got a damned kidnapper running around the county snatching infants from birthing centers."

"Or a ring of them," Granz observed.

"Is the clinic affiliated with U.C. Santa Rita?" Escalante asked.

"No, it's run by independent midwives, like the

Redwood, only bigger. Most of their clients are students, though, so it's partially funded by a grant from the University of California system. Mom's name was—catch this—Bloomy Flowers, a student at UCSR."

"It's your investigation," Mackay said to Granz, "but I think you ought to contact all the private birthing centers in the county. Let them know they might be at risk."

"Already being done," Granz said, "but I'm short of manpower . . . person power. How many more Inspectors can you give me?"

"I'll have Jim Fields contact you."

Minutes later, DA Chief Inspector James Fields had been briefed on the kidnappings. The antithesis of Dave Granz, he was short, stocky, with dark thinning hair and a complexion that bore the aftermath of severe teenage acne, while Granz was tall, slender, athletic, blond and fair. Granz dressed casually and always looked like he was ready to go to the beach, but Fields invariably dressed meticulously in a suit. They shared two characteristics, however: both possessed extraordinary investigative gifts that couldn't be learned at the police academy. And, they were close friends.

To casual observers, with his right coat sleeve gathered up and tucked into the empty space where his hand had once been, Fields looked handicapped. And a lesser man would be. Years before, after a bomb blast ripped off his hand, rather than accept a disability pension, he entered a long, difficult rehabilitation during which he trained himself to function entirely left-handed. Eventually, he was restored to full duty as a DA Inspector and Kathryn's first official act as District Attorney was to promote him to her Chief Inspector.

"I'll spring a few Inspectors loose and send them up to Granz. Meanwhile, I'll offer to personally work with each clinic to see what we can do to step up their security."

"From what Granz said, they don't have any security."

"All the more reason they need my help. I'll do the same at all the hospital maternity units."

Kathryn contemplated. "Keep it low key."

Fields held his left hand out, palm toward his boss. "Don't worry, I'll work directly with their security chiefs. I'll start by making sure they have tape cassettes loaded in their surveillance cameras."

"What about the birthing centers?"

"I'll make sure they're diligent about keeping the entrances and exits locked."

"Jim, I didn't mean to tell you how to do your job."

"No offense taken, Kate. You know I always welcome your input." He laughed softly. "Besides, I know you can't help yourself. It's genetic."

Kathryn laughed, too. "Keep me informed."

Fields turned at the door and slapped the heel of his hand against his forehead. "Now, why didn't I think of that?" he said, and closed the door.

16

"Ms. Mackay?"

"Yes?"

"There's a call for you on line one."

Kathryn glanced at the flashing light on her desk phone, then at the clock. "It's after five o'clock, Jeanette. Take a message."

"He's very insistent."

Kathryn sighed. "Who is it?"

"A Doctor Berroa, ma'am. He called collect and says it's extremely important that he speak with you, concerning a murder case."

"Damn! I don't want to talk to Berroa, he's—" Mackay stopped when she realized Jeanette Whidby had been her secretary for only a few weeks and had no idea who Berroa was.

"Refuse the charges."

Jeanette hesitated. "I already accepted them."

"Okay, put him through, then call Emma's school and tell them I'll be late."

Mackay punched a number and heard the hollow hiss of her recording equipment. "Mackay."

"Thank you for accepting the charges." His soft, Hispanic voice quivered slightly, but perceptibly.

Mackay frowned. Once cynical and arrogant, he sounded like a frightened child.

"Eduardo Berroa?"

"Yes."

"What do you—"

"I'm sorry to interrupt, I don't mean to be rude, but I have only a few minutes. I called to propose a deal that will benefit us both."

"You're in no position to cut a deal, Berroa. I'm going to hang up."

"No, please!" His voice rose. "Give me one minute. If you aren't interested in what I say, hang up, and I will never contact you again."

Mackay thought. "The clock's running."

"I'll withdraw my habeas motion in exchange for a face-to-face meeting with you and Lieutenant Granz."

"My answer to your habeas is already drafted," she lied, then added, "Your minute is almost up."

The DA's recording equipment hissed ominously while he contemplated his answer. "Robert Simmons remains a fugitive, but I know where he is."

"I'm listening."

Kathryn had been involved in an intense relationship with Robert Simmons before she discovered that he had murdered District Attorney Harold Benton, and nearly killed her with massive digitalis overdoses to prevent her from learning of the murder and its motive. He fled to Mexico City to avoid prosecution, then dropped out of sight someplace in Central or South America. Mackay indicted him, then vowed to track him down and bring him to trial. Months later, he sent her a letter saying he loved her, and asking her forgiveness.

"He writes to me," Berroa said.

"I'm still listening."

"The first letter ended, 'Until we meet again.' Does that mean something to you?"

Mackay gasped audibly and her muscles contracted. She placed her palm against her forehead, and leaned on the desk top, pulse pounding and face flushed.

"When did you get that letter?" she asked.

"A long time ago."

"Why didn't you contact me then?"

"I was outraged when you prosecuted me, after I testified against Simmons. I felt you broke the deal I made with you and Lieutenant Granz."

"Involuntary manslaughter was never part of the deal. I only agreed to not charge you with the rapes."

"You're right, but out of anger, I acted as my own lawyer and tried to outsmart you."

"So, what changed?"

"The Nuestra Familia put out a hit on me. They say it's for defiling young Hispanic girls."

"Delicately put, Berroa," Mackay responded. "But you didn't just defile them, you drove them to their deaths."

"Prison is a nightmare, Ms. Mackay. When I get out of prison, I will be deported to Mexico. There I will undergo treatment for my . . . disorder. Nothing like that will ever happen again, I promise you."

"But meanwhile your life is in danger. What do you propose?"

"You and Lieutenant Granz come here. Meet with me. If I help you apprehend Robert Simmons, then we will discuss what I need. Come immediately."

"That's not possible."

"Please."

She pondered her response. "We'll be there tomorrow morning."

"Muchas gracias, Señora. ¡Buen viaje!"

17

"When was the last time you were at Soledad?" Granz asked, breaking the awkward silence.

"A month before becoming DA, when I attended a lifer hearing," she answered, referring to parole hearings for inmates serving life sentences. "I've been sending someone else since my appointment."

"Don't blame you, you've been busy as a peg-legged pirate in an ass-kicking contest."

Halfway around Monterey Bay from Santa Rita, Dave Granz jogged inland, and after a few miles, swung the Explorer south. Highway 1 lay between the Gabilan Mountains on the east and the Santa Lucias on the west, which demarcate the narrow, fertile Salinas Valley that Steinbeck brought to life in *East of Eden*.

As if in answer to his comment, Mackay spread a case file on her lap and pretended to read, but surreptitiously watched Granz. Fourteen miles later, he negotiated around a John Deere tractor pulling a trailer loaded with sprinkler irrigation pipe, onto the off ramp, and crossed over the freeway.

Mackay slid the manila file back into her briefcase. "It's sure ugly, isn't it?"

Granz nodded his agreement. "I hate these places. Maybe I was a criminal in a prior life."

The stark beige buildings of Salinas Valley State Prison rise like an incongruous apparition from the tranquil, lush green lettuce fields just north of Soledad.

Inside a cyclone fence that enclosed the front of the facility's square perimeter, corrections officers lived in tiny single-family barracks. Laundry danced in the brisk spring breeze on old-fashioned cotton clotheslines, while hordes of children played on slides and swing sets, oblivious to the austerity of their environment and the imminent danger if their parents failed to properly perform their professional duties.

Tall razor-wire fences with gun towers at regular intervals separated the inner compound from the housing units. Each tower housed weapons and uniformed officers, who peered down from their perches like hawks searching a Kansas wheat field for errant prairie dogs.

A sign at the prison parking lot entrance warned drivers that their vehicles are subject to search when entering and leaving, and Granz stopped at the kiosk so the officer could inspect their identification. After he logged them in and waved them past, Granz parked next to a white Mercedes-Benz E320.

"I'm leaving everything in the car except my

badge and ID," Kathryn said. "Makes it faster going through security."

"Me, too, I'm not carrying a weapon," Dave acknowledged, dropping his loose change, pocketknife, wallet and detachable key ring into the ashtray after removing the remote. He climbed out and waited until Kathryn closed the passenger door, aimed the remote at the rearview mirror, and dropped it in his pocket when the alarm chirped.

The visitor entrance opened to a small pea-green, tile-floored cubicle which had been chopped in half by a waist-high counter. A Hispanic corrections officer sat at a desk behind the counter, and a huge Caucasian officer with a buzz cut was stuffing manila folders in a metal file cabinet when the door opened. The Hispanic officer stood and walked to the counter. His nameplate identified him as Raul Henriques.

Granz and Mackay presented their badges and IDs, which Henriques inspected carefully, then consulted a visitor log.

"You're here to see Eduardo Berroa?"

"Correct." Granz watched as Kathryn read her waiver form and scribbled her name above a line which read, "The Department of Corrections does not recognize hostages for purposes of bargaining with inmates."

"Makes you feel all warm and fuzzy inside, doesn't it, babe?" he asked.

She was taken by surprise at the unexpected intimacy, and answered, "Dave, shush," reverting to her old, familiar, personal rebuke.

Granz signed his release, then leaned over and whispered to Mackay, "Are you?"

"Am I what?"

He pointed at a sign above the entrance to the inmate visitor section: ALL FEMALE VISITORS MUST WEAR UNDERGARMENTS.

She shot him a stern look. "That's enough, Granz!"

Henriques dropped the waivers on top of an in-basket, handed each of them temporary clip-on badges, and escorted them through a security gate and metal detector, then down a short, narrow hallway, one side of which opened into a gift shop displaying sweatshirts, T-shirts, coffee mugs, stationery and other prison souvenirs.

At the end of the hall, a third officer manned a metal security door that slid open to admit Granz, Mackay and Henriques into an outdoor cage that resembled a dog run. It slammed shut before another door at the opposite end slid open to allow them to pass into a gravel courtyard surrounded by cyclone fences topped with spiral-rolled razor wire.

"Do you want a glass-shielded cubicle?" Henriques asked.

"We prefer a face-to-face interview room."

"No problem," he answered, and entered a room with a small table and four chairs. "Sit on the side closest to the door we just entered."

Momentarily, a second door clanged open and Berroa shuffled into the room with a wiry black officer, who dropped a manila envelope on the table, then removed the chain that connected Berroa's handcuffs and leg irons to a heavy leather belt. He did not remove the restraints themselves.

"Press the buzzer beside the door when you're finished," Henriques told them; then the two officers departed, slamming the door behind them.

Berroa stared at Granz and Mackay for several seconds. When he spoke, his voice cracked, but he made direct eye contact with Mackay, then Granz.

"Thank you for coming. You're the only visitors I've had. I was beginning to doubt that I would ever see another human being."

Mackay pointed at the five-by-eight envelope. "Those are the letters from Simmons?"

Berroa covered them with his hand. "Yes, but I won't give them to you until you promise to help me."

"We'll catch him sooner or later, with or without your help," Granz remarked.

For the first time, Berroa's eyes showed some life. "Perhaps, but without my assistance it will be later rather than sooner, if ever."

"That's why we're here," Granz conceded.

"Simmons is holed up in a Third-World country, and he speaks Spanish. In that part of the world, where the average education is first grade, doctors are gods. No one cares about Simmons' past or his reason for being there, and they certainly won't risk losing their doctor by helping you apprehend him."

"No promises until we see the letters," Mackay said.

"I will have nothing to bargain with if you see them before we make a deal."

"You have nothing to bargain with *unless* we see

them," she said. "They could be from your cousin in Monterrey, Mexico."

Berroa's voice became calm and soft. "I understand your reluctance, Ms. Mackay, but if they are what I represent them to be, will you consider my request?"

"Agreed."

"Good enough." Berroa removed a single sheet of paper, triple folded, and handed the letter to Mackay.

Mackay skimmed it. "It's not dated."

"It came soon after I arrived—it was the first. I can tell by the expression on your face that you recognize Simmons' distinctive handwriting, correct?"

She nodded. "Did you keep the envelope?"

"Of course. It was postmarked Mexico City."

"When did you get the most recent one?"

"Last week."

"Show us the envelope."

Berroa hesitated, then pushed the stack of letters across the table. "The most recent is on top, postmarked two weeks ago at San Jose, Costa Rica. The letter clearly indicates that he is in a village on the North Pacific coast. There are only half a dozen, and they are very small and extremely remote."

Kathryn read the letter. "What do you want in exchange for the letters and your assistance?" she asked.

"First, a transfer to the SHU at Corcoran."

"The Security Housing Unit?" Granz asked.

"Absolutely. As I told Ms. Mackay, Nuestra Familia has a hit out on me. It's just a matter of time before they kill me."

"Okay," Mackay said, "we'll see what we can do. What else?"

"If my information leads to Simmons' apprehension, you ask the governor to commute my sentence to time served."

Kathryn picked up the letters, walked to the door, and pressed the buzzer. "We'll be in touch. If you receive another letter, contact Lieutenant Granz immediately."

"Understood."

18

"Mom, wake up."

"Wha . . . Scotty . . . what . . . ?"

"Why are you sleeping on the sofa in your clothes, Mom?"

"I must have fallen asleep after I fed the baby earlier this morning. He was a little fussy. You're still in your pj's."

"I just got up."

"Good, I'm glad we didn't wake you. What time is it?"

"Nine o'clock."

"Goodness, I promised to take you to baseball practice, didn't I?"

"Yeah, but it's okay, I know you're tired, and Dad's not here to help, and that Jimmy's the most important thing now, and—" Scott Flynt's voice caught in his throat, and he turned away so she couldn't see the tears.

"Oh, honey." Elizabeth Flynt sat up, and patted the cushion. "Come sit here with me for a minute. I know it's hard having a new brother, but no one's more important than you. Jimmy's only two days old, though, and he needs our help, especially for the next few weeks. I can't do it without you, you're so much help."

Scott sniffled. "I am?"

"Sure, you are. You help me hold him, and feed him and everything. Now, why are you crying?"

He scraped the sleeve of his blue and white pajamas over his eyes. "I'm sorry, real men aren't supposed to cry, and I'm the man of the house now, you know."

"Who told you men don't cry?"

"Dad said only sissies cry. I don't want to be a sissy, but I wish he was here and . . . Mom, will you and Daddy live together again?"

She kissed him on the forehead. "I don't think so."

"Even if he promises not to hit us anymore? He told me he won't get mad or hit us ever again, and he really misses us. Will you think about it?"

She looked at her son. "Did you talk to your father? I told you we can't let him know where we are right now. I explained all of this to you!" She waited but when her son refused to make eye contact, she asked, "Does he know where we are, Scott?"

"I guess so."

"How?"

"I called him yesterday afternoon when you and Jimmy were taking a nap. I know you told me not to, but I promised Dad I'd call as soon as Jimmy was born. I couldn't go back on my promise." He started to cry.

"No, honey, you couldn't. Shush, everything's all right." She ran her fingers through his thick brown hair, and stood. "I'll get your brother from my bedroom and drive you to baseball practice."

"Oh, my God!" Elizabeth screamed. She yanked the blanket from the crib and threw it on the floor, then did the same to her own bed, ran into Scott's tiny bedroom and tore it apart as well.

"Scott? Scott!"

"What, Mom?" he shouted from the living room of the small apartment.

"Where's the baby? What did you do with Jimmy?"

"Nothing, Mom."

Elizabeth bent over and looked out the open, ground-level window of her bedroom. "Oh, God," she moaned when she saw the torn screen leaning against the exterior wall beside a plastic recycling bin. "Come here, Scotty, please. Hurry!

"This is very important, honey. What did your father say yesterday when you told him about the baby?"

His ten-year-old eyes filled with tears. "He . . . he said he was coming to see us, but he didn't say he was going to take Jimmy." He paused. "He won't hurt Jimmy, will he, Mom, like he did me and you?"

"I don't know, now be quiet for a minute while I think what to do."

Elizabeth opened her top dresser drawer, pulled a

pair of white cotton panties from the bottom, unrolled them, and removed two crumpled business cards.

"What're those, Mom?" Scott asked.

"Telephone numbers of some people who told me once to call them if I ever needed help."

19

"Let's stop at Hardin Ranch Plaza for coffee." Dave dropped back behind an eighteen wheeler and swung into the slow lane as they approached the North Salinas exit.

"Can't, I'm meeting Miller at the Alexanders' before the kidnapper calls at 5:45."

Granz speeded up. "Oh."

Mackay looked at him. "Why don't you go with me."

"Jazzbo can handle things."

"I know, but I'd rather work with you personally, Dave. I . . . oh, damn." Her cell phone chirped, and she fished it out of her purse.

"Mackay," she answered.

"You probably don't remember me, Ms. Mackay, this is Elizabeth Flynt."

Kathryn raised her eyebrows and whispered to Granz, "Lancaster's sister."

"The Lancaster who murdered her husband?"

Kathryn nodded, and removed her hand from the mouthpiece. "I remember you, Elizabeth."

Elizabeth's voice rose and caught in her throat. "You told me if I ever needed to, that I should call you."

"What's wrong?"

"Bob . . . Bob took my son. I need your help," she wailed.

"Calm down, Elizabeth. Are you sure your husband didn't just take him to work, or to relatives?"

"Yes, I'm sure."

"Did you call the police?"

"No, I've been trying to reach you."

"When did this happen?"

"Early this morning. He tore the screen off the bedroom window."

"Where are you now?"

"At home."

"I can call Redding Police for you."

"I'm in South Cliffs, at three-oh-eight-A Beach Pines Drive. We moved from Redding several months ago."

Kathryn noted that they were passing Española on Highway 1. "We'll be there in five minutes."

Kathryn punched the "End" button on the cell phone and quickly apprized Dave of the situation. With his concurrence, she called Inspector Donna Escalante, and directed her to round up Sergeant Miller at the Sheriff's Department, and meet them at the Flynt residence.

Granz swung the Explorer to the curb and parked behind an old, white Jeep Cherokee covered with a brown plastic tarp. Elizabeth Flynt stood with her left arm around Scott's shoulder, on the front porch of a small, single-level duplex, whose twin garage doors separated the living units.

The sea-foam blue structure was freshly painted, with two identical, tiny, manicured lawns bordered by multicolor marigolds, petunias and pansies, in full bloom. A silver Geo was parked in the A-unit driveway, and a six-foot redwood gate on the east side led to the rear yard.

Elizabeth Flynt's eyes were puffy and red, but when she recognized Kathryn, she smiled feebly and said, "I didn't know who else to call, you were the first person I thought of."

"You were right to call," Mackay answered as they climbed the steps, then added, "Elizabeth, this is Sheriff's Lieutenant David Granz."

"Hello, Mrs. Flynt."

Scott Flynt extended his hand to shake first with Mackay, then Granz.

"I'm confused," Mackay began. "What do you mean Bob took your son? Scott's here with you."

Elizabeth drew in a deep breath. "For a while after you came to Redding, things were better, and I got pregnant. But last February, something must have happened at work because Bob came home angry. When he found out dinner wasn't ready, he beat me up, real bad. Scotty tried to protect me, but Bob threw him up against the wall. I knew if it happened again, I'd lose the baby, and I couldn't let him hit Scotty again, so we left the next day while Bob was at work."

"Why Santa Rita?" Kathryn asked.

"I couldn't go home to Oregon, that's the first place he'd look. Anna Marie still owned this duplex, where she lived before she married Larry Lancaster. Bob had no idea where we were until Scotty called him yesterday."

"Daddy made me promise to call him as soon as Jimmy was born," Scott said defensively.

Elizabeth squeezed his shoulders. "It's okay, honey, Ms. Mackay will find Jimmy and bring him home."

Granz opened the front door, and he and Mackay looked around before entering the bedroom, followed by the Flynts. "Jimmy was in here when he was taken?" Granz asked.

"Yes, in the crib."

Mackay looked outside. "It looks like he climbed through the bedroom window, and left the same way. Do you have a restraining order, Elizabeth?"

"Yes. I have a copy right here." She pulled a thick packet of folded legal documents from a jewelry box and handed it to Mackay.

A car door slammed outside, and momentarily Jazzbo Miller and Donna Escalante entered. After introducing them to the Flynts, Mackay said, "Lieutenant Granz and I need to return to our offices, Elizabeth, but you're in good hands with Sergeant Miller and Inspector Escalante. As soon as you give them descriptions of Bob and Jimmy, and Bob's car—pictures, if you have them—they'll broadcast a state-wide bulletin to all law enforcement agencies to be on the lookout for them."

"Can you stay, too, Ms. Mackay?" Elizabeth asked.

"No, I'm sorry. But, we'll get Jimmy back, I promise."

"You shouldn't make promises you aren't sure you can keep, Kate," Dave said as he pulled the Explorer onto northbound Highway 1, and merged with the dense midmorning traffic.

"I have no intention of breaking that promise," she answered.

20

ALEXANDER RESIDENCE
MISSION HEIGHTS
FRIDAY, 12:45 P.M.

"We couldn't raise two million dollars," Garrett Alexander stated in a calm, emotionless voice, "especially not on such short notice."

The Alexanders sat on opposite ends of the sofa, an innocuous brown Safeway grocery bag on the cushion between them. "We raised half a million. It's in the bag."

Granz slid forward on his chair. "Did you try borrowing from your families?"

"No. If you don't recover the ransom money we'd never be able to pay them back."

"How about remortgaging your house?"

"It's already leveraged."

"You have no other sources of cash?" Mackay asked, looking at Gayle Alexander.

She deferred to her husband, who added, "I'm afraid not. What do we do about the rest of the money?"

"The County will make up the difference from the

Sheriff's and District Attorney's special funds," Mackay told them.

Granz stood. "I'll have Sergeant Miller round up some investigators and sign the cash out of the Treasurer's safe. We'll record as many serial numbers on the bills as we can, and I'll be back with the cash before the kidnapper calls."

Granz rushed in at five-forty with a locking canvas banker's bag and a big suitcase. "Treasurer and Auditor staff helped. Serial numbers are all recorded."

At exactly 5:45 P.M., Mackay's pager buzzed. "It's a Santa Rita number," she said, jotting the number on a sheet of paper, then dropping the pager on the sofa. "Ready?"

Garrett and Gayle Alexander both nodded, but showed no emotion.

"Yep." Granz punched the "Send" button on his specially programmed cell phone, which listened in on Mackay's line, and she dialed the number.

The phone on the other end was picked up on the first ring. "Listen up, Mackay. You have thirty minutes to carry out the first part of my instructions."

"Is Janey okay?" she asked.

"Shut up. I'll talk, you'll listen. If you butt in again, I'll hang up and the Alexanders will never see the kid again. Clear?"

"Absolutely," Mackay answered, nodding at the Alexanders, indicating she was speaking with the kidnapper.

"You are at the Alexanders'?"

"Yes."

"They get the money?"

"Yes."

"Send a cop to the Surf City Bowl at Santa Rita Beach. I won't be there, so don't have him waste time looking for me. Have him remove the object in the coin return slot of the pay phone nearest the men's restroom, and turn it over to you. I'll page you again at . . ." he paused . . . "six-thirty." The line clicked, and the connection was dead.

Granz punched a number into his phone, and when the detective answered, he ordered her to the Surf City Bowl.

"Yes, sir," she acknowledged, then said, "Can you tell me what I'm looking for, Lieutenant?"

"Could be anything. Whatever it is, transport it Code 3 to the Alexander residence."

"What do we do now?" Garrett Alexander asked.

"We wait," Granz answered.

"Excuse us a moment," Kathryn said, motioning Granz to follow her to the foyer.

"What do you think that sonofabitch is sending us?" she asked.

"Depends. If he wants to prove he has the baby, a piece of clothing, or a lock of hair. If he wants to show he means business, it'll be a finger or toe, or an ear."

"Maybe you should meet your detectives outside, so you can give the Alexanders the news yourself, and we can watch how they take it. No matter what the news is, they can't fake a genuine reaction."

"Unless they already know."

* * *

"It's a different number," Mackay observed as she answered the page.

"What was in the pay phone?" the caller said when he picked up.

"A piece of pink baby blanket."

"Do they recognize it?"

"Yes, it belongs to Jane."

"What does the bag the cash is in look like?"

"A large, dark blue, soft-sided Samsonite suitcase."

"Tie a red ribbon in a bow on its handle, and put it on the passenger side of the rear seat of your red BMW."

Kathryn's eyebrows arched. "All right."

"Roll both rear door windows halfway down, and open the front passenger window completely. Before you leave, break out the right taillight, stop light and turn signal lenses but leave the bulbs in. Drive with your headlights on, so each set of lights shows one white light to the rear."

"What if I get stopped by the CHP?"

"Don't."

"Then what?"

"Drive straight down the hill and get on Highway One, South."

"How far do I go?"

"Till I tell you to stop. What's your cell phone number?"

She read him her number, then he said, "I'm watching you, Mackay, and you'll be in the cross hairs of a telescopic sight on a two-twenty-three Winchester rifle. If I even think I see a cop car or anyone following you, I'll kill you and the kid. Got that?"

"Yes."

"One more thing. If I see anything that looks like Granz's Ford Explorer, the game is over. Now, hang up and leave—with the suitcase."

"Kathryn," Granz protested. "Let me assign one of my female detectives to drive your car, and—"

"Lieutenant, may I speak with you for a moment, privately, please?"

Kathryn picked up the suitcase. When she and Dave were in the foyer, out of the Alexanders' earshot, she said, "There won't be any problem if I do as he says, and no one follows me."

"Kate, listen!"

"No, you listen. I know this is your investigation, and if you decide to send a detective in my place, I can't stop you. But you heard what he said. If you do that, you'll endanger the baby's life. We can't take that chance."

Dave paused and looked directly into Kathryn's eyes. "Tune the police radio in your car to secure C-Channel and don't take any chances. I'll monitor your cell phone, too."

She picked up the suitcase with trembling hands. "I'd better go."

21

As Kathryn Mackay eased her car around the Highway 1 on-ramp cloverleaf, her cell phone chirped and she grabbed it from the passenger seat.

"Mackay."

"Good lookin' gray pinstripe suit you've got on, Mackay."

She glanced around and spotted a man wearing a fluorescent orange vest and a yellow hard hat talking on a cell phone, but standing several yards from the remainder of the CalTrans construction crew in the freeway median. "Where are you?"

"Never mind. Drive south, and be ready to hop off the freeway in a hurry."

"Anything else?" she asked, but the line was dead.

Just as she passed the South Cliffs Beach exit, her phone chirped. "Yes?"

"Turn on Española Airport Road and head east to Freedom Road, then pull into the Plug Nickel Saloon parking lot. There's a pay phone there. Wait for me to call."

"What if someone's using it?"

"I hung an out-of-order sign on it. In case one of those drunk rednecks can't read and tries to use the phone, flash your badge—or some tit—whatever it takes." The phone clicked and went dead.

When she pulled into the parking lot, she could hear music blaring through the bar's open door; Willie Nelson singing "On the Road Again."

The pay phone was already ringing. She jumped from the car and picked up the receiver, knocking a half-empty Budweiser can off the shelf. It bounced on the floor, splattering her leg with stale beer and soggy cigarette butts.

"Mackay."

"Get some change and call four-two-two-six-eight-eight-one. If you fuck around long enough to call the cops, I won't answer, and you and the kid die."

She ran back to her car, dumped the contents of her purse on the driver's floorboard and fumbled through the contents with trembling hands. She located several quarters, dimes and nickels and ran back toward the phone booth, but slipped on the muck created by the spilled beer and fell hard onto the gravel. She scrambled around on her hands and knees trying to pick up coins with her bloody fingers, succeeded in finding a quarter, a dime and a nickel, and dashed to the phone.

"What took so long?" he asked.

"Kiss my ass."

He laughed. "I saw you fall through my rifle scope."

She stared at the telephone. *Sonofabitch.*

"When I hang up, count to fifteen, then drive south on Freedom to McDonald's. Pull into the drive-through. Order something to eat, and drive out. Your next instructions are in a manila envelope on the curb. Get going, you don't have much time."

"Welcome to McDonald's, may I take your order please?" the distant, female metallic voice in the order station asked.

Mackay leaned out the driver door window, but before she could say anything into the speaker, a hand grabbed her right shoulder, and a male voice whispered, "Tell the order taker you need a minute to decide what you want."

Startled, she whirled around to confront a man's head in a black ski mask poked through the right front window. Face-black covered the exposed flesh between the ski mask and black turtleneck. His hands, in black leather gloves, rested casually on the door jamb.

"Tell her," he repeated.

"I need a minute to decide," Kathryn said into the order speaker.

"Take your time, ma'am."

"Face forward and don't look at me again," the man ordered. "I'm going to open the back door and take the suitcase. If you don't do anything dumb for a few more seconds, you can drive away. If you do, they'll carry you off in a body bag."

She heard and felt the rear door open gently, heard the suitcase scrape across the leather seat, and the rear door closed softly.

He poked his head through the right front window again. "Wait twenty seconds, then place the food order just like I told you. When you get the food, drive around. I'll call and tell you where to find the kid."

"When?"

"When I get around to it."

When Kathryn looked the suitcase was gone.

Granz' voice crackled over the scrambled C-Channel. "Kate?"

"I'm here."

"You okay?"

"Yes," she replied.

"When's the cash drop?"

"It went down almost an hour ago," she told him.

"Where's the baby?"

She filled him in, then said, "The sonofabitch isn't going to call."

"Shit! Come back in," he told her.

"I'm headed in now."

"Okay."

"Dave, you still there?"

"Yep, go ahead."

She paused. "He could've just had me meet him in some isolated spot and turn over the cash. Why did he run me around and have me answer the phone at the Plug Nickel?"

"You said he was watching you while you were on the phone, right?"

"Yes."

"He wanted you to know he's in control, that he can get to you."

"Why McDonald's?"

"Dinner rush hour. He knew we wouldn't take him down and risk killing a bystander. Safest place he could've picked."

"Sick bastard. See you in a few minutes."

22

FOGBANK INN

"I don't give a shit where, go back to Minneapolis and get a goddamn job."

He snuffed out his Marlboro butt in a pile of coagulated mashed potatoes and gravy, coughed until he gagged, then stuffed a chicken leg into his mouth, stripped the bone, swallowed, and lit another smoke.

"You idiot, I grew up in St. Paul, and worked in Minneapolis for twenty years until—"

He blew a blue smoke cloud in her direction. "Until you got greedy and snatched that first kid?"

Her eyes watered. She waved her hands in a futile attempt to disperse the smoke, then stalked to the window, slammed it open, and turned the recirculating fan on full blast.

"Damn you, that had nothing to do with money." She dropped tiredly back into the cheap motel chair and crossed her arms tightly over her chest.

"He was a crack baby. His mother delivered him on her bathroom floor, then left him lying there while she smoked a pipe. He wouldn't have lived a week with her. You prom-

ised that the adoptive parents would take care of his medical needs."

"Yeah, well if you're so damn pure, why'd you take the money at all?"

She looked at her feet. "I needed it."

"Then you shoulda got a real job. Your antiestablishment crap went outta style with Volkswagen vans, John Denver music and Black Power rallies. An' so did the dumb-ass way you made a livin'."

"It didn't go out of style. I've been a midwife for twenty years, and we're more in demand now than ever."

"Izzat right? Well, if them dumb cunts had went to hospitals, they'd still have their kids. Serves 'em right, goddamn hippies."

"A woman's a hippie because she makes an individual choice about how to bring her child into the world?"

"Fuckin'-A."

She threw a Kentucky Fried chicken wing at him. "Did your mother have any children that lived, you stupid, uneducated, ignorant Neanderthal?"

He ate the chicken, turned the TV volume up, leaned back against the headboard, and crossed his stockinged feet. "Shut up and go pack your suitcase. I'll take you to the airport as soon as this movie's over. It's Gary Cooper in High Noon."

"What if the police figure out who I am?"

"They won't." He coughed, spat a large, stringy yellow glob of phlegm into a Coke bottle, then told her, "We spent five thousand bucks on that phony social security card, passport, driver's license and paper that says you're a certified midwife."

She stood up. "But, what if they do?"

"In that case, I suggest you kill yourself."

She stopped with her hand on the knob of the open door that connected their rooms.

"If the police ever do find me, the first thing I'm going to do is tell them about you."

He sat up, swung his legs over onto the floor, reached under the pillow and pulled out a .25 caliber Beretta automatic with a baffled silencer screwed into the barrel. When he stood and aimed it at her forehead, his hands were steady as rocks.

"I'd kill you right now, but I'd have some explainin' to do to my partner. But, I'll know where you are all the time and if the cops ever get close to you, I'll kill you myself, but not before I blow off your knee caps and elbows, one at a time."

He doubled his fist and punched her in the abdomen. When she fell to her knees, he grabbed her by the hair, lifted her head, and stuck the tip of the silencer in her mouth.

"You'd better hope you never see me alive again, Freddie."

23

Dave Granz switched his television on, propped his stockinged feet on his coffee table, and sipped a Miller Light.

". . . and we're pleased to present this special *Larry King Live Saturday Morning Report,"* an off-camera announcer said, "Now, from CNN's Washington, D.C. studio—Larry King."

The screen faded to a head and shoulder shot of Larry wearing a dark blue shirt with red and blue paisley braces and a powder-blue necktie. He leaned forward on his elbows and glared into the camera with his distinctive hawk-eye stare.

"As a recent father, I am especially concerned by the fact that every year in the United States, almost a million children disappear. About a quarter of them are runaways, or what social scientists call 'throwaways,' which will be the subject of our second special report. Today, we will focus on the half-million children who are abducted by a family member, or kidnapped by total strangers.

"In the last segment of today's report, three experts will share their views on the causes of child abductions, what's being done about them, and what you and I, as parents, can do to protect our own children.

"Our panel will include a member of the FBI's Child Abduction and Serial Killer Unit; a renowned child psychologist representing the Hardiman Task Force on Missing and Exploited Children; and finally, executive director of the Polly Klaas Foundation in Petaluma, California, father of Polly Klaas, Mark Klaas.

"In our second segment, we'll talk to the parents of two missing children. From Pittsburgh, Pennsylvania, Jim and Marge Hendricks, whose six-year-old son Jeremy was abducted two years ago and is presumed dead, although his body was never recovered; and Emily and Lou Swain, whose fourteen-year-old daughter Penny was kidnapped from their Chandler, Oklahoma home six months ago, sexually molested, murdered, and her body abandoned near the high school where she was a freshman honor student. Her murderer has not been apprehended.

"But first, as we indicated at the start of the hour, we'll open this morning's special from our affiliate station in San Francisco, KTVU Channel Two, where Santa Rita County, California District Attorney Kathryn Mackay is standing by."

Granz emptied his Lite beer and walked to the kitchen to get another. "Great idea, Kathryn," he said aloud to himself.

The screen split in half, and Kathryn Mackay's face appeared in front of a San Francisco Bay backdrop, where a sloop in full sail glided across and disappeared behind her head.

"Thank you for appearing on this special edition of *Larry King Live*, Ms. Mackay. Tell us why you're here this morning."

"Thank you for having me, Larry. At around three A.M. last Tuesday morning, an infant girl was kidnapped from her bedroom here in Santa Rita. We're hoping you can help us find Jane and return her to her parents."

"What can I do?"

"I'd like to show a picture of Janey. Perhaps one of your viewers will see her or, perhaps, already has."

"Please do," Larry answered.

The camera moved in to capture a full-screen picture of Jane Alexander in her frilly yellow dress and bonnet. Her tiny hands were clenched and waving above her head, like an Olympic athlete who just won a gold medal.

"Did the kidnappers demand a ransom for Jane's return?" Larry asked.

"They demanded two million dollars. Last night, I delivered the money exactly as directed, but Jane hasn't been returned, nor have her parents or the police heard from the kidnappers."

"Ms. Mackay, are you saying you delivered the money personally?" Larry clarified.

"That's right. The kidnappers insisted on working only with me."

"What do you think went wrong?"

"Nothing went wrong."

"Is it possible the kidnappers had no intention of returning Jane from the start?"

"Unfortunately, Larry, that's a possibility. That's why I'm making this appeal to your viewers."

Larry stared into the camera, which zoomed in for a close-up, erasing Mackay's image.

"*Larry King Live* and CNN will serve as a clearinghouse for information about the abduction of Jane Alexander. Anyone who knows anything that might lead to Jane Alexander's recovery should call my producer at the number scrolling across the bottom of the screen."

Larry swiveled to follow the camera, which had switched to a new angle. "Call any time, day or night, anonymously, if you prefer. I promise that your call will not be monitored by police, and the line won't contain tracing or trapping equipment. Your call will be private, unless you choose to leave your name."

Mackay's image appeared again on the split screen. "Thank you, Larry. Jane's parents and I appreciate your help."

"Thank you, Ms. Mackay. Good luck and God bless Jane Alexander and her family."

The right side of the screen faded and Mackay's image was replaced by a full screen shot of Larry peering into the camera through dark-rimmed glasses that exaggerated the size and intensity of his eyes.

The camera moved back, exposing the sunny Bay background. "Right after this commercial break, we'll talk to the parents of Jeremy Hendricks and Penny Swain, then interview our expert panel, and try to make some sense of these tragedies."

As soon as she was off-camera, Mackay was switched to a private phone line.

"Ms. Mackay, this is Wendy Whitworth, Larry King's producer. We're going to be swamped with phone calls from people who think they might know the whereabouts of Jane Alexander. We need some way to weed out the false alarms."

Mackay described Jane's birthmark.

"Oh, God," was all Whitworth could think of to say in response.

"I'll fax you a picture that shows the birthmark clearly," Mackay promised. "There's no way of mistaking it."

24

"Let's stop, Lulu and I need a blow and a drink of water," Gilbert Isaacs shouted ahead to his wife. He clamped both brake handles tight and slid his Trek mountain bike to a stop in a cloud of dust alongside the dirt trail in Mt. Cabrillo Park.

The black Lab trailing behind on her leash collapsed in the shade of a manzanita bush, tongue hanging out and panting heavily. Gilbert pulled his water bottle out of the frame-mounted holder, squirted a stream at the dog, who drank greedily, then took a deep drink himself.

Maryanne turned around and coasted down the hill to where he sat, set the bike on its kickstand, and plopped next to him. "Sissy. I made it all the way to the top. It's only about ninety degrees, and we haven't ridden more than thirty miles. I was just getting warmed up."

He grinned and squirted water over his head, then the dog's. "I just stopped for Lulu, she's not as young as she used to be." When the dog heard her name, she scooted over and lay her head in his lap.

"Yeah, right." Maryanne took a gulp of water and drew in deep breaths of air through her mouth. "This trail feels like it's straight up, and no one's cleared the growth in years."

"Tough going, all right, but that's the price we pay for solitude and great scenery." He waved his hand expansively. From the steep trail near the top of Mt. Cabrillo, they could see from the turquoise and white shoreline of South Cliffs to the deep, azure water that marked the deep underwater canyon halfway between Santa Rita and Monterey. "You've got to admit it's worth it."

Maryanne made a sunshade of her hands, shielding her eyes from the afternoon sun. "It sure is," she agreed.

They sat in the shade under a scrub oak for half an hour before Gilbert said, "I'll turn Lulu loose for a few minutes, then let's head back down."

He unclipped the dog's leash, and she headed into the undergrowth at a lazy trot. Two or three minutes passed, then she began to wail, a deep mournful cry.

Gilbert laughed. "Must be her genetic memory of the distant past, when her ancestors were wolves."

"Lulu, quiet," Maryanne shouted. "Come."

The dog barked hysterically, and didn't obey. "She sure minds well, doesn't she?" Maryanne stood and started toward the bush. "I'll get her."

She pushed the dense growth aside, but only walked a few feet before she stumbled across the black Lab digging furiously at a freshly turned spot of earth. The hole was a foot and a half or two feet deep.

"Lulu, stop that. Come."

The dog refused to leave, instead, grabbing a piece of pale blue cloth in her teeth and yanking on it.

Maryanne walked over and knelt down to look. What appeared to be the tiny hand and forearm of a life-size doll protruded grotesquely from the dirt. She reached down and touched it and recoiled in revulsion.

"Oh, my God, Gilbert, come here, *please*. Gilbert!!"

Moments later, her husband came charging through the dense scrub brush. Maryanne sat on the ground, legs folded, and Lulu lay beside her, head on her paws, whining softly. "Honey, what's wrong? You scared hell out of me screaming like that. What happened?"

She pointed at the tiny arm, now uncovered to the shoulder, dressed in a tattered pale blue shirt sleeve. "I think it's a baby."

He glanced at the arm and hand. "Nonsense." He stooped over to touch it. "Jesus, it feels just like flesh. It's one of those lifelike, life-size dolls that cry and eat and wet their pants. Here, I'll dig it out and show you."

He dropped to his hands and knees, and found a flat stick, with which he dug in the soft ground. The newly turned dirt came out in large, dry, brittle clods that disintegrated when he dropped them. When the head and trunk were exposed, he leaned over and inspected it closely.

"Jeez, hon, this doll's even got hair and eyes, and—"

Squirming maggots dropped from the eye sockets, nostrils, ears and gaping mouth, and thousands of insects scurried away, agitated by the sudden bright sunlight.

Gilbert dry-heaved. "Oh, my God." He touched the filthy flesh once again, gingerly, as if it might suddenly turn into the plastic and rubber doll that he desperately wanted it to be. Then the stench hit him full in the nose.

25

"I'll get it," Emma shouted. "It's prob'ly Ashley wanting to know if I can go to a movie and sleep over tonight." She sprinted into the extra bedroom that Kathryn had converted to a home office and exercise room.

"Em! Don't run through the house, you'll fall and hurt yourself."

"Okay, Mom," she answered, without losing a step.

Kathryn smiled. Not long ago, Emma's biggest gripe was that they didn't spend enough time together. Now, her main concern was whether she and her friends could go somewhere together without their parents.

"Mom, it's for you," she said in a sorrowful voice, disappointed that it wasn't her friend. "It's Donna Escalante."

Kathryn accepted the phone. "Hello?"

"I hope you don't mind, I told Emma she could call me by my first name."

"I don't mind at all."

"County Comm just paged me. Doctor Nelson is getting ready to autopsy the body of a dead infant that was found buried in a shallow grave in Mt. Cabrillo Park a couple of hours ago. I thought you'd want to know."

"You were right," Kathryn told her. "Contact Doc Nelson and ask him to hold off for half an hour until I can get to the morgue. I want you to work with the S.O. on this investigation, too."

"No problem. Anything else?"

"Who'll be there from the S.O., Jazzbo Miller?"

"No, he's assigned exclusively to the Alexander kidnap. Lieutenant Granz'll handle this."

Damn, Kathryn thought as she kicked off her shoes. "Em, call Ashley and tell her you can spend the night, if it's okay with her mother. I'll drop you off at their house in about fifteen minutes."

"Ya-a-y!" Emma whooped. She grabbed the phone, dashed into her bedroom and started throwing her belongings into a backpack.

"Take your school books," Kathryn admonished.

"Aw, M-o-o-om!"

Kathryn slipped off her gray sweats, and pulled a black Bebe T-shirt over her head with no bra, wriggled into a pair of clean Guess jeans that she removed from her dresser drawer, and laced up her comfortable old Reeboks. Then, realizing she'd probably be at the morgue for several hours, grabbed a black leather jacket from her closet.

Mackay stepped from the elevator in the basement of County Hospital into the morgue and scrunched up her nose at the familiar odor, a putrid and unforgettable mix of disinfectant, formaldehyde, stale air and death.

On the right was a large room containing three stations equipped with stainless steel tables, scales, lockers, sinks, and sluices enclosed in sound-proofed booths, to permit the pathologist to dictate notes.

The cold storage vault where bodies were refrigerated and preserved before and after autopsy was at the end of the corridor next to the staging room, where bodies were weighed, measured and photographed before being rolled on gurneys to autopsy suites.

Donna Escalante and Dave Granz stood in a half circle at the far end of the spotless tile-floored hallway, talking to a man in green, short-sleeved surgical scrubs and green rubber-soled shoes. Mackay smiled when she saw Dr. Morgan Nelson, the County's forensic pathologist, who performed autopsies on behalf of the Sheriff-Coroner.

"Good afternoon, Katie," Nelson greeted her by the nickname that was his special privilege as her closest friend and confidant.

He leaned against the doorjamb of an autopsy suite, peering through wire-rimmed bifocals, with a fringe of short cropped reddish-brown hair sticking out from the bottom of his green skullcap. He motioned with his forefinger for them to follow him into the autopsy suite.

"A few more days and we'd use the VIP suite," he said, referring to the special isolation unit. Fitted with high-capacity extraction fans that directed noxious and offensive gases to an incinerator, it was used to examine bodies carrying infectious diseases or in states of advanced decomposition.

"A boy, no more than a day or two old," he explained. "I've washed and photographed him, and taken full body X rays." He led them to a stainless steel table, on which a tiny purple corpse rested on its back.

Kathryn Mackay was a homicide prosecutor in the trenches for more than fifteen years, and had witnessed hundreds of autopsies, but she glanced quickly at the tiny corpse and turned away.

"Goddamn, I can hardly make myself watch," Granz commented. Years earlier, he was attacked and almost killed by a serial murderer called the Gingerbread Man, and was acutely aware of life's tenuousness and death's finality. Watching Doc Nelson dissect a dead body was almost more than he could tolerate.

"He died seven or eight days ago, *then lay around for a few hours before being buried,*" Nelson declared.

"How can you tell?" Escalante asked.

Nelson picked up a small glass vial and held it out for them to see. "Maggots. Flies lay eggs in the nostrils, mouth, ears and corners of the eyes within thirty minutes of death if the body isn't tightly covered. The flies' life cycle is short, ten to fourteen days. After about a week, the eggs hatch out as maggots, which enlarge and eventually harden into cocoon-like pupae. The adult flies emerge, and the cycle starts again."

Nelson pointed at the dead infant's hands. "Four to seven days after death, the body starts to 'sock' and 'glove'—skin and nails of the feet and hands loosen and begin to shed. I'll confirm my initial conclusion by vitreous humor testing; potassium and glucose analysis of the eye fluid."

Nelson pointed to a pile of clothes on a bench, and the four started slipping into gowns, surgical masks, gloves and paper booties.

"With an infant there won't be much aerosolization, but some airborne particulate material is unavoidable."

He picked up a three-inch black-handled Buck knife, honed it on sharpening paper, then sliced a piece of white copier paper down the middle to test the edge.

"Buck knives work better than scalpels," he explained as he slid on elbow length latex gloves. He covered his nose and mouth with the mask, switched on two intense white overhead lights, pulled down a microphone, and described the procedure as he went.

First, he sliced a V-shaped incision from each shoulder to the abdomen, and a horizontal cut from hipbone to hipbone, then pulled the chest flap over the tiny distorted face, and peeled the skin off the rib cage. With a small battery-powered circular saw, he removed the rib cage to expose the inner organs.

He lifted out the lungs. "Pneumothorax," he observed, sliced them open and inspected them closely as Mackay and Escalante crowded in to watch. Granz lagged behind.

Nelson probed gently at a piece of lung tissue with the tip of the Buck knife. "All infants are born with collapsed lungs, but soon after birth, they begin to breathe and inflate the lungs for the first time. Sometimes, the lungs fail to inflate completely, and the sudden pressure changes in the tissue cause the alveoli—air sacs—to rupture."

Escalante and Mackay leaned over to inspect the tissue, and Nelson continued. "Air leaks out of the ruptures, into the spaces between the pleura—lung lining—and the inner chest wall. If the leakage is slight, it's usually not serious. But, if the air leakage is large, the lungs re-collapse and the infant can't breathe. The condition arises soon after birth, and there are obvious symptoms that any neonatal nurse would recognize instantly; shortness of breath, wheezing, and cyanosis."

"What's cyanosis?"

"The lips and fingernail beds turn bluish. Often, all that's needed is an hour or two of oxygen. In extreme cases, the air that leaked into the chest is removed by inserting a tube into the space and venting the trapped air."

"So, is pneumothorax usually fatal?" Escalante asked.

"Not if the infant's attended to and the condition is diagnosed and treated quickly. This baby was diagnosed and treated, but too late."

"What do you mean?" Mackay asked.

Nelson pointed to the infant's throat. "See that? Someone started to perform a tracheotomy, but never completely opened the windpipe. My guess is that it was a last resort gesture. The baby was already dead."

"How do you know?"

"The incision didn't cause any bleeding."

Mackay contemplated. "Would a certified midwife recognize these symptoms and know what to do?" Mackay asked.

"Absolutely."

Nelson snapped off his latex gloves, stretched them out like huge rubber bands, and shot them at an open stainless steel trash container. They bounced off the wall into the container.

"I shoulda played for the Knicks at Madison Square Garden. They've got the greatest chef in New York at the Play-By-Play restaurant, a young guy named Jim something or other."

"You're too short. And you're white," Granz retorted.

Nelson shrugged. "I coulda been a contender." He slipped off his skullcap and dropped it in the trash can with the gloves. "I'll finish this up later, and get my report to you as soon as it's transcribed."

"How certain are you about the time of death, Morgan?" Kathryn asked.

"It can't be fixed precisely, as you know, but I'd say my estimate of seven days is accurate to within twelve or fifteen hours."

Mackay looked at Escalante, then Granz. "This isn't one of our missing infants. Our first abduction occurred less than five days ago. Dave, I need to talk with you. I'm going to grab a quesadilla at Sophie's on the way home. Do you have time to meet me?"

He looked at her as if he didn't think he had heard correctly. "I'll be there in fifteen minutes, as soon as I wrap things up here."

When Mackay left, Granz said to Escalante, "Inspector, contact every police agency in the state. I want all missing baby reports filed during the past ten days, even if the baby's been recovered."

"What's the point if the baby's been recovered?" Nelson asked him.

"Maybe we'll spot a similar MO."

"Do you want me to rattle the cages of all temp medical placement agencies for nurses and midwives?" Escalante wanted to know.

Granz nodded. "And check NCIC Missing Persons, and the Missing and Exploited Children data bank. Someone must have reported that baby missing."

Escalante contemplated. "Unless the mother threw him away intentionally. It happens, and sometimes they get away with it."

"Not in our jurisdiction."

Dave leaned across the table, clinked his Corona Light bottle against Kathryn's, and took a deep swig.

"Tastes good." He pointed at Kathryn's beer. "You didn't used to drink beer. What's the occasion?"

"Nothing special, I was just thirsty."

"Oh. I hoped it had something to do with us coming to Sophie's together, like we used to when—"

"Dave, don't."

"I screwed up, Kate, I'm sorry. Let's talk about it."

"It was a damn big mistake, and this isn't the time or the place."

"Why not?"

"Because I can't handle it right now."

The waiter brought their food and Dave waited

until he left, then pushed his plate, which was covered with a burrito that weighed at least two pounds, to the side.

"I can't put our relationship behind me, Kate. I still have feelings for you. I thought maybe you felt the same way, and invited me here to say so. But that wasn't the reason, was it?"

Kathryn shoved her quesadilla aside, as well. "No. Berroa called before I left for the morgue. He got a letter from Simmons this morning, postmarked a few days ago."

"From where?"

"Tamarindo, Costa Rica, on the Gulf of Nicoya."

"You've been doing your homework."

"You thought I wouldn't?"

"What I thought was that you'd stay out of it."

"Why? Simmons tried to kill me, not you."

"That's my point. You're too personally involved to handle it."

"I can handle it just fine, and I'm going to bring that bastard back."

"Kate, leave this to the feds to work out with Costa Rican authorities. You can't leave right in the middle of these infant abductions."

"Those are your investigations, not mine. I've assigned my inspectors to you—you don't need me, too."

"I don't want anything to happen to you, Kate. Let me wrap up these investigations, then I'll go. I promise I'll bring him back."

Kathryn stood.

"I have to leave."

"You need to get home to Emma?" he asked.

"She's spending the night at her girlfriend's."

Dave grabbed her hand. "Then spend the night with me."

"No."

"Why, because you're afraid you might admit you still care about me?"

"Because I have to call the airlines."

26

The half empty plane cruised south along the west coast of Baja California, five miles above the deep, sparkling blue Pacific Ocean. Kathryn gazed transfixed as the water drifted past, contemplating the conversation with Dave Granz.

The night before, she booked a seat on a United flight from Los Angeles to San Jose via Mexico City, made hotel reservations, and spoke to an embassy official who arranged for her to meet the United States Ambassador to Costa Rica and his law enforcement liaison early Monday morning.

She was surprised to learn that the liaison was Steven Giordano, who once worked for the Department of Justice. She had worked with him years earlier to identify the Gingerbread Man, the same elusive killer who almost murdered Dave Granz. They became involved in a brief romantic encounter, and she wondered if she would recognize him after so long.

At about 7 P.M., the plane started a gradual descent

above Golfo de Papagayo, made landfall over the white sand beaches of Provincia de Guanacaste, overflew Ciudad Liberia, then banked right and swooped south past Laguna Arenal. The floor of Costa Rica's magnificent Central Valley climbed swiftly toward the airplane, creating a sense that the plane was falling from the sky.

From the starboard side of the aircraft, Kathryn watched a mosaic of sheer cliffs, intense green jungle, rolling hills, dense forests, and checkerboard banana and coffee farms sweep beneath the wing.

At Alajuela, the engines idled back abruptly, the aircraft dropped, and it touched down at exactly 8 P.M. It taxied slowly past palm trees and encroaching jungle growth to the sprawling beige terminal building at Aeropuerto Internacional Juan Santamaría.

The customs area was spotless, modern, light, cool and relatively casual. Kathryn pushed her single bag to the shorter yellow line, reserved for passengers with two bags or less. After her suitcase was X-rayed, she presented the tourist card she obtained at the United Airlines ticket counter in L.A. and stopped at a money exchange to convert two hundred dollars into colones.

It was light and still comfortably warm in the shade beneath the low awning where private cars, shuttles and taxis loaded and off-loaded passengers. Kathryn stuck her head in the passenger window of a shiny clean, bright red Toyota taxi.

"Buenos noches, Señor. ¿Está libre?"

A handsome man in his early twenties smiled. "Sí, Señora."

"Cuánto costaría ir a Hotel Don Carlos?" she asked.

"¿Qué es la dirección de Hotel Don Carlos?"

Kathryn checked her notebook. "Calle nueve a Avenidas siete y nueve, numero setecientos, setenta y nueve."

"Una mil, quinientos colones, Señora."

"Bien," she agreed. The driver got out and placed her bag in the trunk, then started the engine and zipped smoothly away from the terminal, merging into the Sunday evening traffic on Highway 1 south, also known as General Ganas Highway.

The driver kept up a good-natured chatter all the way into the city, but spoke so fast that Kathryn picked up only bits and pieces. She watched the lush country slide past, and dutifully responded whenever the driver paused.

Twenty minutes later, just past Hospital San Juan de Dios, the driver turned onto 8th Street into a beautiful old residential neighborhood, and pulled to the curb in front of an ancient mansion with two huge, fluted columns supporting a vestibule roof that was decorated with discreet brass letters identifying it as HOTEL DON CARLOS.

A porter with white hair, gigantic bushy white eyebrows and dark eyes bowed slightly and picked up her bag. She followed him into the lobby, which more closely resembled a tropical garden than a hotel. The adjacent Garden Lounge and atrium Sun Deck were generously decorated with huge bronze sculptures, most of which depicted native working men—"campesinos"—wearing narrow-brimmed hats, denim trousers, work shirts with rolled up sleeves and open-toed sandals.

Pre-Columbian art and historic knickknacks covered every square inch of interior wall space, except where lush tropical plants sprouted from huge round concrete planters. A gorgeous fern cascaded from a basket suspended from the ceiling. A huge red, yellow and green flower sprouted from the center of the fern, and two long startlingly blue and white striped flowers drooped halfway to the floor, giving the appearance of a macaw hiding in the undergrowth.

"This is lovely," Kathryn said softly, as if she were in a church.

"Muchas gracias," the reservation clerk said. "We are very proud of our hotel."

"I can imagine. Can you tell me where the United States Embassy is?"

"You must go there now?"

"No. Tomorrow morning."

He smiled. "It is not near the hotel. When you are ready to go, I will call you a taxi. It will take about twenty minutes."

"Thank you. Is there someplace nearby where I can get something light to eat?"

"Sí, Señora, our kitchen is open. Perhaps you would like to relax in the Rattan Room and enjoy your complimentary cocktail while you listen to music and browse the menu."

"I'd like to freshen up first," Kathryn said, "then come down. That sounds very nice."

The clerk snapped his fingers for a bellman, who appeared, placed her suitcase on a cart, and took the key. "As you wish, Señora. If you require anything, please call me. My name is Federico, I am also the concierge."

Fifteen minutes later, Kathryn dropped, exhausted, into a high-back rattan chair, sighed and crossed her legs.

A waiter appeared from nowhere, startling her when he said, "Buenos noches."

"Buenos noches. May I see a dinner menu, please."

"Yes, of course. May I bring you a cocktail?"

She considered. "I'd like a cold beer."

"Sí. I suggest Cerveza Imperial, Costa Rica's finest."

"That sounds good."

After two beers and a plate of tapas, Kathryn retired to her room, showered, then put on a robe and lay on the bed and fell asleep.

27

Monday morning, Kathryn Mackay's taxi driver weaved in and out of the bumper to bumper traffic, coping with precarious situations by accelerator and horn rather than brakes, but the bright red taxis were clearly outnumbered and outmaneuvered by hundreds of smoke belching diesel trucks of various sizes. For sheer brazen disregard for safety, however, no one came close to the motorcyclists, who darted among the cars, taxis and trucks trailing huge blue-gray exhaust clouds, in total disregard for life, limb, and law.

By the time the taxi stopped at the yellow passenger unloading zone in front of the embassy, Kathryn was clinging to the grab strap on the back of the driver's seat, and she gratefully paid the driver, then climbed out onto the sidewalk.

The United States Embassy in San Jose occupied most of an entire city block in a sprawling beige concrete building surrounded by manicured lawns, palms, and profuse tropical plants, trees and shrubs.

The grounds were elevated several feet above street level by a solid bulkhead, topped by an eight-foot fence of square cement posts and black, vertical wrought iron bars.

As Kathryn climbed the flagstone steps into the embassy grounds, she spotted numerous strategically situated closed-circuit cameras, antennas and microwave dishes on the roof of the main structure, reminding her that while technically sovereign U.S. territory, the embassy was, nonetheless, in the midst of the Third World.

A two-story high, canary yellow facade on which the round brass embassy seal was affixed, demarcated the main entrance, which was locked and guarded by two marines in full dress uniform. Kathryn presented her passport and wondered if she was being watched by a security guard inside the embassy.

The marine sergeant greeted her politely but officiously, checked her passport and name on a guest list, then unlocked the thick glass door and admitted her with a crisp salute.

Inside, the reception area was spacious and bright, but sterile. A receptionist checked her passport again, led her to a large set of double doors, knocked, then escorted her into the ambassador's office.

Three men stood, and the man behind the large wood desk extended his hand. "It's a pleasure to meet you, Ms. Mackay. I'm Manuel Ortega, United States Ambassador to Costa Rica."

Ortega was short and slender, with jet black hair that belied his age, which Kathryn guessed to be late fifties. A beautiful, expensively tailored light gray suit complimented his flawless olive skin, intense dark eyes, and the bright smile that struck Kathryn as more formality than friendliness.

"May I present Señores Alexis Arguello of the Costa Rica Attorney General's office and Steven Giordano, my liaison to Costa Rican law enforcement, and consultant to the Costa Rica Federal Police Academy on criminal profiling," Ambassador Ortega said, indicating the other two men, Arguello first.

"Welcome to Costa Rica, Señora," Arguello said as he gripped her hand briefly. The lawyer wore a light blue summer suit and was unremarkable in appearance except for his handlebar mustache and dark, almost black complexion.

When Kathryn first met Steve, he was tall, broad shouldered and trim waisted, with large brown eyes and premature gray in his dark brown hair. His hair was now heavily streaked with gray, but otherwise he appeared not to have aged.

Once, at age seven, after meeting him for the first time, Emma told her mother that Steve ". . . has a sad look on his face when he doesn't know you're looking." He still did. It was that inexplicable sadness and gentleness in his eyes to which Kathryn had first been drawn, if not attracted. That came later.

Giordano grasped her hand. "Ms. Mackay and I met several years ago, Mr. Ambassador, when we worked together to apprehend a serial killer who was terrorizing young women in her jurisdiction."

Kathryn noted that his voice hadn't lost the Little Italy New York accent. "I'm happy to see you, Steve; it's been a long time." Then she turned to Ortega, who sat behind his desk, but did not invite them to follow suit.

"My aide advised me of the purpose for your visit, Ms. Mackay. I've assigned Mr. Giordano to you for as long as you need him, to interface with local law enforcement officials, and to help with travel and other arrangements at Tamarindo. Señor Arguello will be your official contact with the Costa Rican Attorney General, who must approve all extradition requests, and will obtain a court order to return Dr. Simmons to the United States, in the event he is apprehended."

"Thank you."

"You're welcome. Now, as you can imagine, on a Monday morning my calendar is very full. My secretary will arrange a place for you to work. Use it as long as you like, and please let my staff know if we can do anything to help."

After they were settled in a small conference room, considerably less ostentatious than the ambassador's office, Arguello asked, "You have a certified copy of the arrest warrant for Robert Simmons, Señora?"

Kathryn removed the warrant from her briefcase and handed it to Arguello, who inspected it closely.

"This appears to be in order. Why do you think Robert Simmons is in Tamarindo?" he asked.

"He mailed a letter from there about two weeks ago."

"I see."

Giordano explained. "There's a medical clinic at Tamarindo that services most of the villages and tourist areas of the western Nicoya Peninsula. It's very remote. Not many doctors are interested in going there, so medical care is a highly prized and jealously guarded commodity in such communities. Simmons could easily practice medicine there, no questions asked. It's a good place to start."

"Still profiling, I see," Kathryn observed.

Giordano shrugged.

"I shall have a Costa Rican arrest warrant prepared for you before you depart. Present it to Tamarindo police when you arrive, and they will serve it and take Dr. Simmons into custody," Arguello told them.

He stood. "Now, if you plan to arrive there before the end of the day, you must leave." He stood and shook hands with Kathryn. "It was a pleasure meeting you. I wish you good luck at Tamarindo."

28

"It's about a hundred seventy miles to Tamarindo," Mackay said. "Can we drive?"

"Most of the roads are impassable this time of year. An embassy driver will take us to Pavas Airport, where we can catch a flight, if you're up to it."

She looked at him skeptically as he opened the limo door. "What do you mean, if I'm up to it?"

"They fly single-engine planes, and the pilot's likely to be the mechanic or accountant."

"Is it safe?"

He held his hand out palm down, and rocked it back and forth. "Occasionally an engine fails and they make an emergency landing. Crashes aren't usually fatal, but they go down in remote spots and it takes days to ferry in repair parts on horseback. And, the air is rough over Costa Rica, so we'll have a roller coaster ride all the way. The scenery is spectacular, though."

The limo pulled up to a cyclone fence, behind

which an ancient Cessna Skylane with faded blue and white paint rested over a puddle of oil.

Giordano walked to the locked metal gate and whistled, and a man slid out from under the plane on a mechanic's creeper, flipped away a glowing cigarette, and sauntered to the gate. He wore greasy green coveralls and a San Francisco Giants ball cap.

Giordano showed his identification, they exchanged a few words in Spanish, and the man nodded.

"We've got seats," Giordano told Kathryn, "but we have to wait in line."

She pointed to three men queued up at the gate. "How many people does the plane carry?"

"Five. Those are the other passengers."

"Why wait in line?"

"In Costa Rica, it's the national pastime. Some companies hire people to do nothing but stand in lines for them. If we don't, we won't get on that plane."

"We're flying in that thing?"

"Yep. And the guy I talked to is the pilot, mechanic, ticket agent, air traffic controller and airport manager. His name's Enrique Hernandez."

A few minutes later, Hernandez stepped from a blue metal structure that looked like a portable garden shed, wearing fresh dark blue trousers and a chambray shirt with Travelair's logo on the left pocket.

"Pilot uniform," Giordano observed.

He strolled to the gate, which he unlocked and swung open. "Buenos dias," he greeted them, then in English, "Good morning. Welcome to Travelair flight eight-three, for Tamarindo. The fare is eleven thousand colones, which I will collect as you weigh in, please."

Each of the first three passengers paid, then stepped on an old-fashioned drugstore scale, weighed themselves, picked up their bags, weighed again, and were directed to walk across the tarmac to the plane.

When Mackay approached the gate, she asked, "How much baggage am I allowed?"

"Twenty-five pounds, Señora, but your briefcase and overnight bag weigh less. Proceed to the aircraft, por favor."

Hernandez tossed the bags in the tail section of the fuselage without securing them, then seated the passengers, one in the copilot seat, two directly aft, and Giordano and Mackay in the rear seats. He ordered everyone to buckle up, flipped several switches, stuck his head out the window, shouted, "Clear!" and pressed the starter button.

Nothing happened.

"Puta!" Hernandez muttered to himself. He removed his shoulder harness, ran to the front of the plane and lifted the cowling. Mackay heard a loud thump, then Hernandez climbed back into the pilot's seat.

"Clear!"

The engine coughed, sputtered, shuddered, and caught. He opened the throttle until the plane began to move, then taxied across a bumpy, grassy patch onto the end of a crudely paved runway marked "15" and jammed the throttle to the dashboard. The plane lifted off just before the runway disappeared into the jungle and began a steep, climbing right turn.

"Should the plane be so loud and shake so much?" Mackay shouted at Giordano.

Hernandez unfastened his shoulder harness, turned around, and draped his arm over the pilot seat back.

"This is normal, Señora. I repaired the aircraft's engine. Por favor, relax and enjoy the flight."

"I don't mean to be rude, Señor, but shouldn't you turn around so you can see where we're going?"

The pilot laughed. "Señora is cautious, but there is no other traffic. We shall fly over those mountains ahead to Golfo de Nicoyo, then turn northwest toward Tamarindo. Now, I turn around."

When the plane leveled off at cruising altitude, the pilot throttled back. Below, Mackay saw only dense jungle interrupted by the occasional clearings of homesteads or tiny villages.

Passing the coastline, the pilot banked gently right. The engine coughed, sputtered, stopped and the plane dropped like a rock. Hernandez calmly cranked an overhead lever and punched the starter. The engine fired and the plane surged forward.

Hernandez turned around. "Lo sciento, I forgot to switch fuel tanks and ran out of gas for a moment."

A few minutes after the plane turned left over Isla Chira, Hernandez announced, "That is Santa Cruz below. We will begin our descent into Tamarindo."

They touched down on a narrow gravel runway. There were no airport buildings, but when the plane coasted to a stop, a white Volkswagen van pulled alongside the plane and two men climbed out.

"Policia," Giordano said.

In their late twenties, both men were dressed in dark blue uniform trousers and light blue shirts. The taller man smiled continually and had on a jaunty black beret, dark blue vinyl jacket, and a low-slung revolver in a leather clamshell holster.

The second had a neatly trimmed mustache and a scowl. Just under his right elbow, his automatic pistol rode in a high-rise holster fastened to an army-green web duty belt. A baton and handcuff case hung from the left side, and his shiny leather jacket was zipped halfway up. He kept his thumbs tucked in the duty belt.

Giordano exchanged a few words in Spanish and handed them the arrest warrant. The taller officer nodded, glanced at Mackay, slid the van door open, then slammed it behind them.

"The policia don't speak English," Giordano explained, "and they had no idea we were coming, or why, until I gave them the warrant. They'd tip Simmons off if they knew."

The van bounced and jostled its way over the deeply rutted dirt road, dodging the major pot holes, land slides and mud puddles, eventually reaching the outskirts of a village.

A sign beside the road said, TAMARINDO.

"I thought it would be bigger," Mackay commented.

Giordano looked around. "This is the old village. The tourist area is more modern. It has a couple of hotels, a few restaurants, a small shopping district, and the medical clinic. But, it's primitive."

The van raced past a run-down residential area, where tiny thatch-roofed houses backed directly up into the jungle, whose tentacles clawed their way onto the roadway. The dirt turned to gravel and the gravel to asphalt as they approached, and suddenly a modest, beige-pink adobe village appeared, profusely decorated with tropical plants and flowers.

Most of the buildings were occupied by small restaurants and sidewalk cafés with colorful awnings and outdoor patios, or shops with hand-painted advertising signs hanging from their facades, and carts full of handcrafted products displayed in front. The street was narrow and rough, but there were a few new sidewalks.

Suddenly, the van swerved into a parking lot and stopped beside a modern, single-story building constructed in the same Mediterranean style as the other commercial structures. The Costa Rican flag rippled in a light breeze from a pole in front of the building.

The Clinica San Marino building sat next to an art gallery. Over the door, a large white sign with stenciled blue block letters flanked by bright red crosses read, TAMARINDO EMERGENCIAS.

After they exited the van, Giordano spoke to the officers in Spanish. "I told them to have the receptionist call Simmons to the front counter, where he will be taken into custody," he told Mackay.

"I think they ought to go in unannounced and arrest him before he gets suspicious, or runs."

"Respect for his position prevents them from

barging into his private office. Besides, there's no reason for him to be suspicious, and if he did run, where would he go? You saw what it's like getting into this place. There's nowhere to run."

"I don't know, I still think—"

"From this point on, we have nothing to say about it. They make the arrest their way."

Inside, Mackay positioned herself to the side of the door leading from the waiting room to the rear of the building.

The police officers spoke briefly to the receptionist, who nodded and pressed a button on her phone, waited for a few seconds, spoke into the handset, and dropped it back in the receiver.

Momentarily, the door opened and Robert Simmons strode into the reception area wearing a white lab coat. The receptionist pointed toward the three men standing at the counter and Simmons glanced at them.

"Señor? ¿Que pasa?" he asked the tall officer.

Mackay walked around the end of the counter.

"It's been a long time, Robert. These men are here to arrest you."

At first, he looked around as if to flee, then smiled at her. "I knew you would eventually come, Kate, but I thought you would be alone."

"You thought wrong."

29

Kathryn gazed through the dense palms surrounding the patio lounge at the Tamarindo Hotel. Beyond the trees, the frothy turquoise Pacific lapped onto the beach, then hid in the sand. She imagined laughing and splashing in the surf with Emma and Dave.

"What's on your mind, Kate?" Giordano asked.

She swirled the straw colored wine around her glass. "Simmons," she told him. "I won round one, but I won't be satisfied until he's in prison."

"That sounds personal."

The arrest warrant had charged Simmons only with Benton's murder, and she considered telling him the entire story, but didn't.

"Benton wasn't just my boss, Steve. I take it personally when someone murders one of my friends."

"I understand."

"What happens with Simmons now?" she inquired, more to change the subject than to obtain an answer.

"Provincial officials will transport him to San Jose,

where the court will appoint an attorney to handle the extradition request. U.S. prisons are comparative country clubs, so prisoners typically waive extradition."

"It sounds like there's a 'but' in there someplace."

"The U.S. Embassy must file a formal extradition request along with a diplomatic note pledging to not add charges, or impose a stiffer sentence than approved by the Costa Rican Attorney General. Their AG probably won't grant extradition if the charge carries a possible death sentence, because capital punishment was abolished in Costa Rica."

"It wasn't abolished in California."

"True, but Costa Rican law precludes extradition before his lawyer approves the wording in the diplomatic note. If it includes the words 'death penalty,' that won't happen."

"So if I seek the death penalty, they won't extradite him?"

Steve shrugged. "It could be appealed, but it'd take years to wind its way through provincial court, appeals court, the court of cassation, and the Supreme Court. And, the U.S. wouldn't pursue it anyway, due to diplomatic considerations."

"Why not? He's a murderer."

"Because he's a doctor in a country where most people never receive medical care during their lifetime. They could assign him to a remote prison, where he can provide free medical care to the poor."

"What if I appeared before the Attorney General?"

He shook his head. "If you want to prosecute Simmons, you'll need to tone down the sentence."

"Damn." She set down her glass. "I've got to catch the evening flight to San Jose."

He pointed toward the bar, where Enrique Hernandez was chatting with a woman in a bikini and drinking a piña colada.

"Oh, great. It was bad enough with him sober," Kathryn commented.

"The flight's been canceled."

"Why?"

"The plane's engine won't start. They're flying in a new magneto tomorrow morning."

"Where do I stay?"

"Here at the hotel."

He caught the bartender's attention and gestured. "Let's have more wine."

"No, thanks."

"Then, let's eat," he suggested.

Suddenly, a bloodcurdling scream shattered the quiet.

"What was that?" she asked.

"Howler monkeys, in the trees."

"Are they dangerous?"

"They're not aggressive, just loud. What they want is a handout, so they'll hop down here and grab the scraps when we leave."

Kathryn ordered fish stew, and Steve's catch of the day was a broiled filet of an unknown species. After dinner, the sun dropped below the horizon and painted the sky in extravagant purple, orange and red. They watched an iguana sun itself on the brick walkway beside the bar, and settled into an uneasy quiet.

Steve broke the silence. "What happened, Kate? When we worked on the Gingerbread Man case, I thought we made a special connection."

"After Sacramento recalled you, it seemed like nothing ever happened between us, Steve. Working together day and night, it seemed all right at the time, but it wasn't real."

"So, you just forgot about me?"

"Not entirely, but I believe relationships have just one window of opportunity. If you don't seize it, it's gone for good."

"There's never a second chance?"

"I honestly don't know." She paused, then stood. "Now, I think I'll check into my room."

"I'll call the embassy and have a driver pick us up tomorrow afternoon and drive you to Alajuela to catch the late-night flight back to Los Angeles."

"Thanks. I'll see you tomorrow."

30

The pink while-you-were-out note taped to Mackay's office telephone read, *Call Lt. Granz @ S.O.* She punched in a four-digit number and waited.

"Granz."

"It's me."

"Nice of you to come back from Costa Rica," he said without preamble. "Can you meet with me, Escalante and Menendez?" he asked, referring to Roselba Menendez, the criminalist whom most of law enforcement considered the best technician at DOJ.

"When?"

"As soon as possible."

"Be here in thirty minutes."

Menendez was short and slightly overweight with sleek, short black hair, perfect olive skin, a slight Hispanic accent, and denim Capri pants with a cotton cardigan. She distributed glossy 8x10 black-and-white photographs. "One shows the tire track casting from the Alexander kidnap scene, the other from the fire road near the dead infant's grave at Mt. Cabrillo Park." She pointed at one photo then the other with a manicured, bright red fingernail.

"Same tread pattern, same wear characteristics and same unique road hazard details. The tracks were made by the same tire, on the same vehicle. The Department of Transportation requires tire makers to mold identifiers into the sidewall. We captured the DOT number in the casting. The last three digits, oh-three-nine, identify the manufacture date as the third week of 1999."

"About how many tires were manufactured that week?" Escalante asked.

"Thousands, but the other numbers and letters tell us it was manufactured by Bridgestone at its Nashville, Tennessee plant. It's a low-noise Dueler, comes on semi-off-roaders, size 245-70R-16. It's original equipment on some GMC and Chevrolet Suburbans."

"We need to find that particular vehicle for it to do us any good," Escalante commented.

"Yeah," Granz agreed, "but it must have been built and sold in April or later. I'll contact General Motors and request that they search assembly records for all Suburbans built after the third week of March and equipped with Bridgestone Duelers. They can trace vehicle shipments to dealers, and warranty files will identify the buyers."

"There's one more thing," Menendez continued. "The shoe prints that Sergeant Yamamoto photographed at the Alexander crime scene were made by two identical pairs of size twelve Nike Air Cross Trainers, but they were too new to ID the specific shoes."

"Anything else?" Mackay asked.

Menendez shook her head. "If you don't need me any longer, I need to get back to the lab."

"Have the Alexanders heard from the kidnapper?" Mackay asked after Menendez left.

"Not a word," Escalante said.

"Have you identified the dead infant?"

"Aaron Mitchum," Granz told her, "abducted from Laguna Birthing Center in San Diego. The parents are estranged, so SDPD had been concentrating on the father, who has a long history of domestic violence."

"Speaking of batterers, how about Robert Flynt?" Mackay asked.

Escalante leaned forward. "As soon as we determined that he didn't kidnap the baby, I called him to see if he could help. He said, 'Tell that fat, ugly cow I was married to I hope they never find the kid, it'll save me a lot of child support.' What an asshole!"

"What was the MO in San Diego?"

"Same as Redwood and University," Granz answered.

"Any matches in the NCIC databases?"

Escalante shook her head. "Not yet."

Mackay gazed at the ceiling. "I don't understand how Jane Alexander fits in. All the others were taken from birthing centers, but her mother said she was born at a hospital."

"Not true," Granz corrected. "You asked if the baby had been finger and footprinted at the hospital when she was born, and she said, 'I'm afraid not.' I'll follow up."

Mackay nodded. "Anything new on the University Center abduction?"

"No temps were working when the Flowers infant was taken, but they use the same nationwide agency—MedTemps," Escalante answered. "Immigration laws require temp agencies to prove the employee's identity with at least one document that contains a photo. Most employees use a passport or driver's license."

"What did Fraley use?"

"A passport, but the feds say it's a forgery."

"Figures."

"We caught a couple of breaks. MedTemps copied her passport photo, and DOJ ran it through DIPS."

The Digitized Identification Photograph System was started by the Department of Motor Vehicles to digitize driver's license photos, which were then archived as computer files. The crime lab could digitally scan photos of unidentified persons and match them to files in the DMV database almost as reliably as fingerprints.

"Won't help if she's never been digitized. What's the second break?"

"She listed her name as 'Fraley, Monica F.' on the employment app. Women her age—fifty-one—often use their maiden names in some way, or their ex-married names if they have children. I figured the 'F' means something."

"Not much to go on, but maybe you'll turn something up," Mackay commented a bit skeptically.

"I did. Costa Mesa MedTemps placed a 'Fraley, M. Fredericks.' at Laguna birthing center just before Aaron Mitchum was abducted. She used a driver's license for identification. They didn't photocopy it, but they recorded the number," Escalante told her. "Another forgery."

"But, you think it's the same person?"

"I called Gretchen Potter at Redwood Clinic, who said Fraley insisted on being called 'Freddie.' San Jose MedTemps is searching for Fraley's previous placements. Hopefully, we'll locate a personal reference, next of kin, or someplace she considers home."

"Can they flag her name in the national database and notify us of future referrals?" Granz asked.

"Already done," Escalante assured him. "They'll check every day. If she's placed, we'll know within twenty-four hours."

"Assuming she uses the same agency, the same name, and the referring branch updates the database promptly," Granz added. "But it's a lot more than we had before."

"None of the parents are rich enough to blackmail except the Alexanders, and their baby wasn't returned even after the ransom was paid. What's the motive behind the abductions?" Escalante mused.

"Figure that out, Inspector, and we'll be halfway to catching the perps," Mackay observed.

Donna Escalante leaned on her elbows, chin resting on her hands, examining copies of Monica Fraley's passport and employment applications that San Jose and Costa Mesa MedTemps faxed to her.

She slid them next to one another, tapped the data in the identical box on both employment applications with a pencil tip, marked each space with a yellow felt-tipped high liter, then picked up the phone.

When the San Jose MedTemps receptionist answered, she asked for Lillian Graham, the manager.

"Inspector, you don't need to call, I'll check every day and let you know if Monica Fraley's name comes up."

"Would you check another name for me?"

"Sure, what?"

"Fredericks, or maybe Frederick without the 'S,' but the same first name; Monica."

"How soon do you need this?"

"Can you check while I hold?"

"Sure, I'll boot up my computer."

After a pause, Graham said, "There are fifteen or twenty Fredericks in the system. No Monicas, but three listings with the first initial 'M.'

"Can you access the applications on-line?"

"Sure, and so can you. We want all MedTemps offices to keep abreast of our midwives' experience. They're posted on the World Wide Web."

"Check the birth dates on the San Jose and Costa Mesa applications," she suggested, shoving them across Granz's desk. The boxes were circled in yellow hi-liter.

"They both say October three, forty-eight."

"Right. And, all three that I downloaded off the

Internet show the same DOB: ten-three-forty-eight, too."

"What's the most recent?" Granz asked.

"Just a couple of days ago."

"Where was that one input?"

"Cleveland, Ohio," Escalante told him.

31

"Yeah?"

"It's me."

He muted the television, which was tuned to the Turner Classic Movie Channel, extricated himself from the woman, and grabbed the phone.

"Jesus Christ, I can't even get laid in peace. Whadaya want?"

"The cops found her."

He covered the mouthpiece, swung his bare legs over the side of the bed and sat up. "Go get me a beer. Then take a shower and wash that stinkin' thing."

He lit a Marlboro, dragged deep, formed an 'O' with his lips and blew out a smoke ring which floated to the ceiling and disbursed. Then he sucked in a second lungful, and exhaled.

"How th' fuck do you know?"

"I have a source."

"Shit!" he said into the phone.

"You picked her—she's become a problem—you take care of it. Now."

"Suck my dick, bitch. You ain't paid me all my fuckin' money yet."

"Knock off the gutter language, and listen carefully. Take care of this problem immediately, or I'll hire someone else to do it. Then I'll take care of you."

The woman handed him a Coors. He slid his hand up her thigh, buried his thumb in her pubis, sniffed it, then pinched his nose and pointed toward the bathroom.

He listened for the shower, then said into the phone, "You ain't got the balls to kill me."

He laughed at the incongruity, wheezed, coughed, spat a string of mucus into an ashtray, and lit a fresh Marlboro.

"I won't have you killed. I'll simply drop your name in a few places and you'll be back in prison before you know what happened."

He swallowed half the beer, dragged on the cigarette, doused it in the mucus-filled ashtray, and lit another. "Where's she at?"

"Cleveland."

"I'll catch the next flight outta San Jose."

"I knew I could count on you. And, Michael—she cannot be allowed to talk."

"She's got to talk." Mackay scrutinized the employment application forms. "The birth date's the same on all of them, and so is the handwriting. Fredericks is Fraley, and she's the key to recovering those infants."

"Looks like it," Granz agreed. "Parma Heights MedTemps placed her at Cleveland Clinic's new birthing center. They're expanding alternative health care services. I faxed her passport photo to Cleveland PD. They confirmed her identity and home address. She's being surveilled, but they won't move until I get there."

"Do you want to take Escalante?"

"No, I'll have plenty of help."

"Call me as soon as she's in custody and I'll fly to Cleveland. Meanwhile, I'll have an arrest warrant issued and fax it to you."

32

"You got the arrest warrant, Captain?"

"Your DA faxed it a couple of hours ago."

Cleveland PD Detective Captain James Lamarr was a black man with a bald spot, a slight paunch and a toothy smile. His gray slacks were wrinkled, his shirt sleeves were rolled above the elbows, and the red tie was pulled down several inches below his loose collar. A damp stain spread from his armpits.

"Fredericks is working swing shift, Lieutenant. Do you want to take her down at the clinic or bust her tonight at home?" Lamarr asked.

Granz shook his head. "Nothing to gain by waiting."

Lamarr wove the unmarked Caprice through the traffic at the I-71, I-90 merge, drove north, then exited onto Ontario Street.

"That's what I figured. Birthing center's next to Children's Hospital at Carnegie and East Ninetieth.

Three patrol backup units are on the way." He picked up the dash mike. "Green units acknowledge."

"A-fourteen, six-three-three green at Carnegie Avenue exit."

"Six-eighteen green at East Ninetieth exit."

"Six-oh-one green at Skyway exit."

"Ten-four."

"We'll park in the main lot and go in the front entrance to Building M," Lamarr informed Granz. "The birthing unit's at the far end and there aren't any rear exits."

Lamarr and Granz climbed out of their Caprice and headed for the clinic entrance.

"Motherfucker! Those are cops, I can smell the cocksuckers," he mumbled to himself. He ground out the Marlboro with the toe of his boot, and sat back down in the rented Ford.

He entered eleven numbers into his cell phone, and punched the send button. When she answered, he told her, "I'm at Cleveland Clinic, but so are the cops."

She contemplated. "Do you have any ideas?"

"They've gotta book her, so I'll stake out the jail. I'll get a chance sooner or later."

"You'd better hope it's sooner."

"I told you not to threaten me."

"Just do it."

The receptionist protested, but Lamarr flashed his badge and kept walking. Halfway down a wide, spotlessly clean tile-floored corridor, he stopped and put his hand on the handle of a door marked NURSE & MIDWIFE STATION.

"Ready?"

"Let's go," Granz answered.

The room was chopped into small cubicles where neonatal nurses and midwives shuffled paperwork, plus a central area strewn with file boxes, chairs, and a table with a coffee maker, cups and an empty donut box.

Four women, two black and two white, wearing green uniforms, glanced up as the men entered, then went back to their paperwork.

"Good evening," Lamarr said. They all looked up, irritated at the interruption. "I'm looking for Midwife Fredericks."

One of the white women was short and stocky, with long gray hair pulled back and clipped with a beret. She wore wire-framed glasses that accentuated green eyes and dark bushy eyebrows. She wore no make up or jewelry, except for a man's Timex watch and a string of multi-colored beads. Her name tag read, MONICA FREDERICKS, CERTIFIED MIDWIFE.

"I'm Captain Lamarr from Cleveland Police, and this is Lieutenant Granz from the Santa Rita California Sheriff's Department. We have a warrant for your arrest."

"They just took her into the jail to book her," he said into the cellular phone. "You called me too damn late, nothing I could do."

"Will she talk?"

"Not right away, I scared the shit outta her."

"They'll wear her down eventually."

He laughed. "I know, broads can't stand up to that heavy shit."

She ignored the sexist comment. "What do you plan to do about it?"

"The jail chow hall's in a separate building. I'll take care of her when they move the female inmates over for breakfast. She won't never get to eat."

"She'd better not."

"Fuck off."

33

Granz switched on the recorder. "It's nine-eighteen A.M., June seventeen, nineteen-ninety-nine. Present are Santa Rita County Sheriff's Lieutenant David Granz, and Monica Fredericks, who has previously been advised of her Miranda rights and has agreed to talk with me. Is that right?"

The 23-story Cuyahoga Justice Center Tower and Corrections Center occupied an entire city block demarcated by West 3rd, Ontario, St. Clair and Lakeside. The old jail connected to a new building called Jail-2, which housed an arraignment court, offices, kitchen, dining hall, the women's detention unit and several interview rooms.

"There's been some sort of mistake." Fredericks wore a standard-issue jail jumpsuit and appeared tired, but unafraid. She leaned forward on a small table barely big enough to hold the coffee jug, paper cups, a box of tissue and Granz' microcassette recorder.

"Then, clear it up so we can both go about our business. Tell me your birth date."

"October third, nineteen-forty eight."

"What kind of work do you do?"

"I'm a certified midwife."

"Married?"

"My husband passed away almost a year ago."

"Children?"

"I have a sixteen-year-old son, Jimmy."

Granz hid his surprise. "It must be difficult raising a teenager by yourself."

"He's institutionalized."

"What do you mean—institutionalized?"

"He was born addicted to crack cocaine, and his mother abandoned him at birth. Soon after the adoption was final, we found out something was wrong."

"What do you mean, 'wrong'?"

"He barely felt pain, he'd stick his fingers into electrical sockets, or touch a hot stove, and never even wince."

She hesitated, then continued. "He fell asleep banging his head against the wall. Once it was so loud the neighbors called the police. He's in a state hospital."

"In Cleveland?"

"No, Minnesota."

"I'm sorry," Granz said softly. "Where do you live, Ms. Fredericks?"

"Ninety-two–sixty Quincy Avenue."

"How long have you lived there?"

"Not very long."

"Before that?"

"I was traveling in my motor home, working now and then to earn gas and food money."

"Alone?"

"Yes."

Granz leaned forward and interwove his fingers on the tabletop. "Did you work at the Redwood Alternative Health Clinic or the University Birthing Center in Santa Rita, California?"

She folded her arms over her breasts. "Maybe I should call a lawyer."

"That's up to you."

Granz waited. "I didn't hear your answer, Ms. Fredericks."

"I've never been in California. I ran out of money in Kansas City, and headed back toward Minneapolis. At the last minute, I decided to come to Cleveland."

"Don't you want to be near your son?"

"He's noncommunicative—it's a waste of time. My husband left a lot of bills. I'm avoiding creditors."

"Do you remember when you left Kansas City?"

She thought for several seconds. "I think it was Wednesday, June tenth. I drove to Des Moines, Iowa."

Granz leaned back and crossed his right leg over his left. "Did you keep your gasoline and food receipts?"

Fredericks cleared her throat. "Why would I do that?"

"How about credit card charge slips?"

"I told you, we had bad credit. I paid cash."

"You said you left Kansas City because you were broke. Where did you get money for gas and food?"

"I worked for a couple of days in Des Moines," she answered quickly.

Granz smiled. "If you'll give me the name of the birthing center you worked for, I'll confirm it, and you'll be on your way."

She stared at him. "I can't."

"Can't what?"

"Tell you the name of the birthing center."

"Why not?"

"The owner paid me in cash, under the table, so the IRS wouldn't know, and no taxes would be withheld."

"I promise I won't give the IRS anything, so why not give me the name?"

"I agreed I wouldn't. Besides, she's had her own tax problems and will deny I worked there. It'll be my word against hers."

Granz shrugged. "How did you locate jobs while you were traveling. Did you register with an agency?"

"No, temporary work is easy to find."

"Have you ever registered with an agency?"

"Not until I got to Cleveland."

Granz flipped the notebook pages. "MedTemps confirms that no one named Monica Fredericks had registered before this week. But Monica Fraley has," Granz added softly.

She sat heavily, without removing her eyes from Granz. "I won't answer any more of your questions."

Granz phoned Mackay from Lamarr's office and filled her in. "Are you flying to Cleveland?" he asked.

"Absolutely. I get to Cleveland at six-forty-five this evening."

"Should I book you a room at the Marriott?"

"Yeah, I'll see you in a few hours."

34

"The plane was late and the cab must've taken the long, scenic route from the airport." Kathryn Mackay was wearing black Guess jeans and a black shirt, and still looked hot. She set her wineglass on the table in the lounge of the Marriott Hotel.

"I'm exhausted, and how can you hear anything except that racket from the television?"

Dave Granz had changed into faded Levis, white Reeboks, and a black Salinas Harley-Davidson T-shirt that said UNLEASH YOUR BEAST on the front.

"I don't *want* to hear anything else, it's the bottom of the first inning of the Indians-A's game from Oakland, and the A's just scored three runs."

"Don't you guys ever get tired of watching football? Let's move to another table, where we can talk."

He started laughing. When he couldn't stop, she started, too.

"What's so funny?" she asked. "I feel like a fool laughing when I don't understand the joke."

"You're what's so funny. The Indians and A's are baseball teams. Football doesn't start until September."

"Same thing as far as I'm concerned."

He grabbed his beer and her wineglass and pointed to a rear table. "Let's move back there away from the TV, I was getting tired of breathing the cigarette smoke, anyway," he suggested, then started laughing again.

"It's a simple mistake that anyone could make," she said in mock indignation.

When they sat down, she said, "I need you to bring me up to speed on the Fredericks interview before I file the extradition request tomorrow morning."

The table had a bowl of peanuts on it, and Dave tossed half a dozen into his mouth, washed them down with beer, then did it again.

"Dave, eat more slowly and savor the peanuts. You can't enjoy them if you eat the entire bowl in two or three mouthfuls," Kathryn admonished.

Dave popped another handful of nuts in his mouth. "I enjoy them this way and I already had a mother, Kate. She taught me how to eat and I don't need any more lessons." He took another swallow of beer and dribbled it on the Harley logo.

He wiped his shirt with a bar napkin. "Maybe I wasn't paying attention during that lesson."

This time, Kathryn laughed. "Stop it, we need to talk."

He shoved a cassette tape player across the table. "Listen to the Fredericks interview first."

She took a sip of wine and nibbled at a peanut,

then began listening. "Dave, you're driving me crazy eating those peanuts. If you're so hungry, go order us some hamburgers."

When he returned from the bar, the bowl of peanuts was gone, but he decided not to notice.

She switched off the recorder.

"Couldn't get her to cop out," he complained.

Kathryn swallowed a bite of food and another sip of wine. "Great burger. The San Jose MedTemps owner and the midwife at Redwood can ID her."

"I'll punch holes in that bullshit alibi about driving from Kansas City to Cleveland when the Sweet and Flowers kids were snatched. That'll put her tit in a wringer."

"Damn it, Dave, stop talking like a sexist!"

"Sorry. Can I interrogate her again back in Santa Rita? We're no closer to finding the babies or her accomplice than we were."

Kathryn thought for a moment. "She didn't invoke her right to an attorney?"

"No."

"If she only invoked her right to remain silent, under certain circumstances, further interrogation is okay."

"What circumstances?"

"You re-advise her, she waives, and you don't ask about the same crime."

"What good does that do?"

"Ask about the kidnapping in San Diego and the death of the Mitchum infant."

Dave smiled. "Very good, counselor." He touched

his glass to hers. "How about another glass of wine?"

She looked at her watch. "I'm tired. I think I'll go to my room, get out of these clothes, watch some TV, and unwind before I go to bed."

"And put on that scruffy old robe?"

She laughed. "You know me too well."

"How about a back rub to help you relax?"

She looked at him for a long time. "I don't think so."

"Why not?"

"Jeez, Dave, don't you ever give up? When we were . . . oh hell, I don't know what we were . . . but when we used to see each other, a back rub usually led to something more intimate."

"So?"

"So, you're starting to wear me down and I'm not sure I could resist."

Dave laid two twenty dollar bills on the table, stuffed the stub from the bottom of the tab into his wallet, and handed her a room key that looked like a credit card.

"You're all checked in." He stood and held out his hand, which she accepted, and pulled herself to her feet.

"We have adjacent rooms," he told her.

She tried to free her hand, but he hung on. "I said adjacent, not adjoining, Kate. You're virtue is safe."

"Not with you."

Their bodies touched as they rode the elevator to the fifth floor. At the door to Kathryn's room, he pulled her close and, encountering no resistance, kissed her.

She felt him stir against her abdomen and, to her surprise, she returned the kiss, but eventually pulled away.

"We can't neck here in the hall like teenagers," she said.

"Sure we can."

"I'll let you watch TV with me for a while if you promise to behave."

He raised his right hand. "Scout's honor."

She unlocked the door and swung it open. "Don't give me that Boy Scout line, you phony, you were never in the Scouts." She looked around the room. "Oh, what's that?"

She walked to the writing table, where a dozen red roses were arranged in a crystal vase.

"There's no card. Where did they come from?"

"I had them sent to your room."

"That was sweet, Dave, thank you," she said. "But, you still have to sit on that end of the couch, I'll sit on the other. Let's see what's on TV."

While she flipped through the channels, Dave broke the seal on the in-room bar. Before she could object, he popped the cork on a bottle of Domaine Chandon champagne, and handed her a glass, then plopped on the sofa beside her and kicked off his shoes.

Kathryn sipped her champagne, sighed deeply, turned sideways on the sofa, and stretched luxuriously. When she did, her foot kicked Dave on the thigh, but before she could apologize, he picked her feet up and set them on his lap.

"I've missed being together, Kate."

She felt him grow firm, but didn't remove her feet from his lap. "Dave, don't."

He fell quiet, but continued to rub the bottom of her feet. She sipped her champagne, poured them each a second glass, and they watched *Law & Order*, in silence.

When it was over, Kathryn said, "Wouldn't it be great if real police work was like that? A crime is committed, the police catch the bad guys, and the DA puts them away, all in less than an hour."

"No, because we wouldn't get to spend an evening together at the Marriott Hotel in Cleveland, and you wouldn't get a foot massage."

She drained her glass. "Is the other massage offer still open?"

"You know it is."

"I'll be right back."

She returned wearing a new cotton nightgown, and lay on her stomach on the blanket Dave spread on the floor. He had turned off the lights, but a soft blue neon glow from a distant sign flooded the room.

Firmly and slowly, he worked the deep tissue of her shoulders, sliding his hands down her arms, back up to her shoulders, down the spine to her buttocks where he lingered, then back up to the neck, kneading with his palms as he proceeded.

"Are you asleep?" he asked.

"Almost."

"This would feel better if you weren't wearing the gown," he suggested tentatively. When she didn't respond, he tugged at the bottom of the gown. She raised her body enough for him to slide it over her head, but remained on her stomach.

He started at her feet, sliding a finger between each toe, massaged the tops and bottoms in firm circles, worked up her ankles and kneaded her calves so deeply it was almost painful, and rotated and pressed his thumbs deep into the backs of her knees. Slowly, tantalizingly, teasingly, he massaged her outer thighs.

Then she felt his hands move her legs apart so he could stroke the inner thighs; close to, then closer, but never touching her most private parts. Highly aroused, she rolled over.

"Dave, I told you . . . I shouldn't . . . this isn't right, but I want you so much."

"I want you, too, babe," he whispered hoarsely.

She pulled his shirt over his head and ran her fingers through the hair on his chest, then raised her head, put her mouth over his right nipple and sucked.

"Oh, babe, I've missed you," he groaned.

Her fingers found the buttons on his levis. When he was naked, she grasped his swollen penis and stroked while his finger searched briefly, then slid inside her.

She moved with his hand. "Yes," she whispered.

He knelt between her legs and kissed her vulva, teasing her with his tongue as she guided his head with her hands. When she felt close to orgasm, she lifted his head and whispered, "Not yet, I want to be on top."

He lay on his back, and she knelt over him, knees beside his chest, reached down and placed the tip of his penis barely inside her.

He arched his back and pushed, but she pulled away. "Not yet," she said. "Let me. Slowly."

He cupped her breasts and pinched the nipples between his thumbs and forefingers and watched her slowly lower herself onto him, gradually consuming him entirely.

"Oh, that's good," she whispered. "But this will make it better."

She leaned over and picked up the champagne and glasses. Dave began to thrust, but she held him firmly to the floor. "No."

He propped himself up on his elbows and accepted the half-full glass. She clinked her glass against his and raised it to her lips, then began to slowly rise and fall.

Just as she swallowed the last of her champagne, she whispered, "Now, Dave, come now with me."

He groaned and spent himself deep inside her. Simultaneously, she spasmed, and dug her fingernails into his shoulders, but he didn't notice.

Later, as she lay with her head on his chest, she said, "I never intended for this to happen between us, again, Dave. I don't know what it means."

"Are you sorry?"

"No."

He kissed her on the cheek. "Me, neither. I love you more than ever. I want us to be together again, Kate, this time with a permanent commitment."

She remained silent.

"Can we discuss it?" he asked.

"I don't know."

Reluctantly, he got up and dressed, then ran his

fingers through her hair. "I should go back to my room, we both have some thinking to do."

"I'll see you tomorrow morning for breakfast."

When he was at the door, she said, "Dave?"

He turned.

"Thank you."

"For what?"

"For knowing when to leave."

35

"Don't read this until you get home."

Dave handed Kathryn a beige greeting card-size sealed envelope, which she accepted without comment and slid into her purse. Then she gave the Continental Airlines counter agent her ticket, and waited for a boarding pass.

Both Ohio and California law incorporate the Uniform Criminal Extradition Act, so on advice of her attorney, Monica Fredericks waived extradition, and Kathryn Mackay's request was first on Cuyahoga Superior Court's Friday morning calendar.

By the time Judge Roscoe Sweeney reviewed certified copies of the complaint and the California arrest warrant, took testimony, and issued an Ohio warrant and extradition order, it was too late for Dave to accept custody of Fredericks and make the flight, so he drove Kathryn to the airport to catch the 3:00 P.M. plane to San Francisco.

When she got her boarding pass, he followed her

to the security entrance to the boarding gates. She dropped her bag onto the conveyor and kissed him on the cheek.

"Kate, I—"

She placed the tips of her fingers on his lips. "Don't say anything, we'll talk soon," she promised.

She passed through the metal detector, grabbed her bag, and merged with the crowd. He watched her disappear before turning and slowly heading back to the parking lot.

The plane didn't lift off the tarmac until almost four o'clock, but as soon as they reached cruising altitude, Kathryn pulled the envelope out of her purse and set it on her lap. She contemplated briefly, then tore it open and removed a flowery greeting card with TO MY SPECIAL LOVE on the front. It was blank inside, except for the handwritten note.

Kate—Let's try again. Don't say no before thinking about it. I won't mention it again unless you do.

Dave

Kathryn ate the small salad but left the chicken breast dinner untouched. She bought a mini bottle of Fetzer chardonnay and after dinner, reclined her seat and closed her eyes momentarily, awakening when the flight attendant announced the plane's descent into San Francisco International.

Friday night traffic on I-280 was a nightmare of fleeing commuters, elderly vacationers in Winnebagos, and smoke-belching diesel trucks. Two accidents reduced four lanes to one near Palo Alto, and traffic over the summit from San Jose was clogged by the summer migration from the hot, smoggy Santa Clara Valley to the ocean beaches.

At the crest of the hill, Kathryn picked up her cell phone and dialed her neighbor Ruth. Since she was already asleep, Kathryn decided to bring Emma home early the next morning.

She stopped at FroYo Xpress near the mall for a pint of chocolate frozen yogurt, and got home just before eleven o'clock, changed into dark blue sweats and dropped onto the sofa.

Spooning yogurt directly from the carton, she grabbed the TV remote and started channel surfing, but stopped when Channel 7 News co-anchors Steve Wallace and Arliss Kraft appeared.

Wallace stared into the camera. "Good evening, I'm Steve Wallace."

"And I'm Arliss Kraft." She tapped a stack of papers on the desk top to align the edges. "This is Channel Seven Eleven O'Clock News for Friday, June eighteenth."

The camera pulled back for a waist-up shot of Kraft and Wallace.

"Parents and the public are increasingly worried about the recent spate of infant abductions. Police have been unable to solve these crimes, so hospitals and birth centers are taking steps to protect themselves. Here with that report is James Walter. James?"

Kathryn leaned forward and set the yogurt carton on the end table.

The scene faded, then the image of a young reporter with a goatee and bushy dishwater-blond hair appeared. He wore slacks and a tie, but no jacket, and his shirt sleeves were rolled up above the elbows. Beside him, a slender man in his late fifties, in a security officer uniform, waited patiently. A brightly lighted main hospital entrance was visible behind them.

"Arliss," Walter began, "I'm here at Salesian Sisters Hospital with Security Chief Gary Pritchett." He turned to the officer. "Chief Pritchett, what are you doing to ensure the safety of newborn babies?"

Pritchett looked directly into the camera with intense gray eyes. "In addition to roving security patrols and closed circuit cameras that record all activity throughout the hospital, we've implemented Code White procedures," Pritchett said.

"Can you explain Code White?"

"It's an emergency missing patient procedure."

"Are you saying someone is missing?"

"No, this is a precautionary as well as a recovery protocol. First, all entrances and exits are closed, locked, and their electronic sensors activated. The door alarms are hardwired to a control panel at our central security office to notify the watch commander instantly if security is breached anywhere in the hospital. Everyone, including doctors, nurses and other medical staff, must enter the hospital through the main entrance, which your viewers can see in the background."

Walter glanced around. The camera zoomed in briefly to show two armed guards, then drew back. "Is that a metal detector?" he asked.

Pritchett nodded. "It's similar to those at airports,

courthouses and federal buildings. We verify the identity of anyone claiming to be hospital staff, and require identification from all visitors, then record their names, addresses, and the name of the patient they're visiting. We log them in and out and account for everyone in the facility at all times. Identical security is in place at the rear delivery entrance."

"I see."

"Dedicated telephones in the pediatrics and OB-GYN units automatically dial a security hot line as soon as the receiver is picked up. I've doubled the guards inside the hospital and increased motorized patrols outside on the grounds and parking areas."

"How long will Code White procedures be in place?"

"Until the kidnappers are caught. Patient safety is our number one concern right now."

On cue, the camera zoomed in to a head and shoulder shot of the reporter. "Unfortunately, Steve and Arliss, private birth centers are less optimistic. Here's that portion of my report, which was recorded earlier."

The scene shifted to Walter standing on a lawn with Evelyn Franchette, in front of the sign that read, REDWOOD ALTERNATIVE HEALTH CARE—PREGNANCY COUNSELING AND BIRTHING CENTER.

Franchette was the taller of the two, and her gray hair piled on her head made her look even bigger. She still wore a sweatshirt, Levis and open-heel Birkenstocks.

"Ms. Franchette, exactly what do you do here?"

She squinted into the lights. "We provide families

an alternative to the impersonal and expensive care provided by hospitals for childbirth."

"Isn't it risky?"

"Definitely not. I work closely with the woman's doctor and provide dedicated, well-trained, caring staff."

"I didn't mean medically. You don't provide much in the way of security, do you?"

"If the police did their job, it wouldn't be a problem," she answered. "Four babies have been stolen in the past week and a half and so far, nothing's been done."

"You're saying the police aren't doing their job?"

"Those babies should be back with their parents. But one is dead and who knows the fate of the others."

She drew in a breath. "They've ruined me."

"What do you mean?"

"I haven't had a client in almost two weeks. Expectant parents are terrified, so they're going to hospitals whether they want to, or can afford to, or not. Birthing centers like mine are shutting down."

"There you have it, Steve and Arliss," Walter said in closing. "I spoke with several birth center operators who voiced similar complaints about the police. Now, back to you at the Channel Seven studio."

Arliss and Steve shook their heads at each other sadly, then Wallace gazed into the camera. "Channel Seven News will continue to update this story, and bring you law enforcement's response as soon as the District Attorney and the Sheriff's Chief of Detectives return our calls."

"Sports with Rob Schmidt is next, following this break," Kraft said.

Kathryn carried the melted yogurt into the kitchen and poured it down the sink, then picked up the phone.

After the answering machine message tone, she said, "Dave, this is Kathryn. Call me at home as soon as you get this message, no matter what time it is. We need to talk." She paused, then said, "About business."

36

CLEVELAND, OHIO
SATURDAY, JUNE 19

At five o'clock, he checked out of his hotel and ate breakfast at a downtown diner. While he ate, he surreptitiously smeared sausage grease on his uniform, followed by egg yolk, coffee, cream, maple syrup, hash browns, butter and orange juice.

After breakfast he pushed the huge wheeled stainless steel collection container down St. Clair Avenue and glanced casually at the Justice Center parking area as he passed. At West 4th Street, he stopped and knelt, first with one knee then the other, and saturated each in a pile of fresh dog feces that still steamed in the chilly predawn air.

Farther down toward Old River Road, he wrestled the container up the steps and knocked at the front entrance of a nondescript building. He could have worked from the roof of several other buildings with unobscured views of the Justice Center, but chose this one for ease of access. The security staff was young blacks drawing minimum wage, and there was only one on duty at a time.

The snoozing guard glanced up when he heard the noise, rose from his chair and ambled to the glass double doors.

He waved and pointed at the container and whispered encouragement under his breath. "Shuffle on over here, you dumb cocksucker, today's your lucky day."

The guard's silver nameplate identified him as Edward Atlee. Atlee peered through the door, spotted the coveralls, on which had been stenciled CLEVELAND DEPARTMENT OF SANITATION JOE, *shook his head and unlocked the door.*

"Man, whatchu wont this time a the day?" He scrunched up his nose. "Sh-e-e-e-i-t, don' you fuckers never wash them coveralls? Tell the truth, Joe, I oughta be kickin you smelly honky ass outta here."

"No problem, Edward, I've got a special wet garbage pickup on the fourth floor, so I'll just tell the building super you wouldn't let me in. He'll be real happy when he comes in Monday morning and finds the building stinking even worse than me."

"Aw man, fuck!" The guard stepped aside to allow him to push the garbage can through, then relocked the doors. "Follow at a distance, trash man, elevators be 'round the corner."

As soon as they turned the corner, out of sight from the street, he jammed a ten-inch Buck hunting knife to the hilt into Atlee's back, twisted the blade, stuck again, then pulled it out.

At first Atlee didn't seem to notice, but then he staggered and turned around and tried to say something. Nothing came out of his mouth except a soft groan and bloody froth, before he collapsed facedown on the shiny tile floor.

He stepped over the rapidly expanding pool of blood

and wiped his knife blade on Atlee's shirt. "You should be more polite to your guests, Edward, and avoid racial epithets."

Once on the roof, he removed the coveralls and pulled a Winchester carbine from the can. He attached the telescopic sight, then screwed an air-baffled silencer into the barrel. Cautiously, he propped the rifle on the waist-high wall and sighted it in, making minute adjustments to the sights until it was exactly as he wanted it.

Finally, he loaded an ammunition clip, jacked a round into the chamber and propped the rifle against the wall, lit a Marlboro, tuned his Casio portable TV to a vintage movies channel, and settled back to wait for the women to cross the outside space for breakfast.

At 6:45 A.M., a female deputy escorted the female inmates to breakfast through a new inside corridor. Male inmates entered the new dining room via an underground tunnel whose origin was the original jail.

He checked his watch. He had been incarcerated in the Cuyahoga County Jail years ago, and knew the women should have been escorted across the parking lot to breakfast at least half an hour earlier. Something was wrong.

His cell phone chirped. "What?!"

"Has the problem been resolved?" she asked.

"I'll let you know when the job's done."

"Make it soon, or I'll find another technician."

"Fuck off."

At 8:15 A.M., after breakfast, Granz signed Monica Fredericks out of Cuyahoga County Women's Detention Facility. Two uniformed female deputies escorted them to the rear door that opened onto the parking lot while a third waited in an unmarked car to drive them to the airport.

Halfway to the car, Fredericks stumbled and fell, and Granz reached out to help by grabbing her arm, but he couldn't stop her from collapsing onto the pavement.

He noticed she didn't move, then realized that his face and neck were warm, wet and sticky.

Then he spotted the blood, mucus, tissue and bone fragments.

When he rolled Fredericks over, her entire head was missing above the eyes and great spurts of bright red blood gushed from where her skull had once been.

He dropped to his stomach and drew his service weapon, searching frantically from side to side, trying to locate the source of the fire. He expected to be hit any minute.

Before he could shout for help, the deputy jumped from the car and sprinted to where Granz and Fredericks lay on the asphalt. She assessed the situation, drew her weapon, crouched and ran back to the car, yanked the microphone from the dashboard, and radioed for assistance.

Within minutes, the jail parking lot and adjacent streets were saturated with cops trying to figure out who had shot whom, from where, and why.

Someone covered Monica Fredericks' grotesque head with a rag.

* * *

He flipped the Marlboro butt over the wall and watched it float to the ground.

From his vantage point, the Justice Center looked like a scene from The Keystone Kops. By the time they got around to checking the building, he'd be thirty thousand feet above Nebraska.

He laughed aloud, coughed deeply and spat a lunger on the roof, laughed again, then packed the rifle into the garbage can, put on his coveralls and rode down the elevator.

He stepped carefully around the pool of blood emanating from Edward Atlee's corpse. "When you get wherever you're going, say hello to Monica, Eddie. She's a dumb cunt, but what the fuck—she ain't no dumber than you, even if she is a honky."

After he broke the rifle down and packed it into the carrying case which was secreted at the bottom of the can, he slipped off his coveralls and let himself out, locking the doors behind him.

He strolled down Old River Road, where he tossed the coveralls in the river. Then he caught the RTA Red Line at the Ritz Carlton, checked in at the Continental ticket counter, smoked a Marlboro, and boarded the Continental Airlines flight to San Francisco.

37

"Oh, God, we're on fire!" Kathryn Mackay struggled to get out of her seat, but was paralyzed. Flames streaked past the airliner's window.

"I know," Dave said.

An alarm clanged and the cockpit door slammed open, but it was empty. The plane pitched forward into a steep nose dive, and started to windmill, flinging Emma from her seat. She smashed headfirst into the first-class bulkhead. Blood gushed from the gaping wound, and her left arm bent backward grotesquely, the jagged bone poking through the skin.

"Mom, help!"

Kathryn looked around the cabin frantically. "Why are you all wearing parachutes?"

"We're bailing out," Dave told her. "The plane's going to crash."

"What about Emma and me?"

"There aren't enough parachutes."

She grabbed Dave's arm, but he removed her

hand, then started the engine on his Harley-Davidson Low Rider. "Good-bye, Kathryn," he said, and rode out onto the airplane's wing.

"Take Emma with you!"

"I can't, she doesn't have a helmet." He waved, then disappeared in the darkness.

"Mom! Help!"

The alarm bell rang again, louder, then again. Kathryn reached out and knocked the telephone and lamp off the nightstand.

"Emma!" She held the phone to her ear.

An unfamiliar female voice asked, "Is this District Attorney Kathryn Mackay?"

"What? I, oh, I'm sorry, I must have been dreaming. Yes, this is Kathryn Mackay."

"Ms. Mackay, this is Wendy Whitworth, calling from *Larry King Live.* I know it's only six A.M. there on the West Coast, but this is very important."

Kathryn swung her still trembling legs over onto the floor. "How can I help you, Wendy?"

"At the end of last night's *Larry King Live Late Edition,* we broadcast pictures of the Alexander infant. This morning, I received a call on the special information hot line from a woman named Deborah, who says she knows something about the baby."

Kathryn wrote down the number, repeating it aloud as Whitworth read it to her.

"I returned her call. She wants you to call her as soon as possible."

"You think she's legit?"

"She described the birthmark."

* * *

Kathryn threw on an old robe, made coffee, then carried it into the spare bedroom that served as exercise room, guest room, and home office, and sat at her desk.

She booted up her desktop computer and logged onto the Internet. When her home page appeared, she clicked on "People Finder," then selected reverse telephone listing and keyed in the phone number Whitworth gave her. The reply came back, "Cherry Hills, Colorado, MANOFF, G&D."

The phone picked up on the first ring.

"Hello?" the woman's voice sounded anxious.

"This is District Attorney Kathryn Mackay calling from Santa Rita, California. Wendy Whitworth said you wanted to talk to me."

"I saw a picture of Jane Alexander on *Larry King Live*. She looks similar to my adopted daughter, Amanda."

"I'm sure many women with adopted daughters fear the same thing, Mrs. Manoff."

"How did you know my last name?"

"I looked your phone number up on the Internet," Kathryn told her. "Does your husband agree with you?"

"Gary doesn't know I called. I'll show you Amanda's picture if you want to see it."

"How?"

"I scanned a photograph into my computer. I can attach it to an e-mail in PDF format."

Kathryn waited a minute, then retrieved two messages. One was junk mail. She opened the other, from deb@Hotmail.com, into Adobe Acrobat Reader. The photo showed the baby's face and neck, but only a glimpse of her upper torso. Although the picture quality had degraded from Internet transmission, a deep purple discoloration was discernible on the left side of the baby's upper chest. Mackay clicked the maximize icon and enlarged the image.

"There are some similarities," she said cautiously, "but it's hard to say from only this one photograph. Do you have any others?"

"No," she paused. "What should I do?"

"Blood typing or DNA tests can prove your daughter isn't Jane Alexander."

"How?"

"They compare the baby's DNA to the parents. Do you have a family doctor?"

"Yes, but as I said, my husband doesn't know."

"I could speak with him," Kathryn suggested.

"He's not home."

"The only way to be sure is to have her tested."

She hesitated. "Can you arrange it?"

Kathryn flipped through the Yellow Pages. "Yes. Stay near your phone, I'll call you back."

"When?"

Kathryn quickly counted the hours. "Tonight."

Kathryn called the Cleveland Marriott Hotel, but Dave Granz had already checked out. She made reservations on a morning flight from San Francisco to Denver, and was stuffing clothes into an overnight bag when the phone rang.

"Yes."

"Kate, it's me."

She stopped. "Something's wrong, I can hear it in your voice."

Kathryn listened for ten minutes without interrupting. When he finished, she asked, "Are you all right?"

"Fredericks was in my custody, and I was responsible for her safety."

"There was nothing you could have done."

"I know you're right, but Jesus—"

"Do they know where the shot came from?"

"Could've been a dozen places. Cleveland PD's checking all the buildings out, but it's slow-going, most are office complexes that are closed on Saturday, and they have to contact someone to let them in."

"How much longer will they need you there?"

"I can leave now, why?"

She briefed him on Deborah Manoff's call. "Can you meet me in Denver?" she asked.

"Sure. Does she know we're coming?"

"No, I told her I'd call later, I was afraid she'd take off."

"Okay, I'll contact Cherry Hills PD and request that they set up surveillance at her house."

"Good."

"As soon as I book a flight, I'll call your cell phone so we can set up a time and place to meet in Denver," he said.

"I'll leave as soon as I arrange for Em to stay with Ruth."

"I'll make room reservations for us," he volunteered. "One room or two?"

She thought about it.

"Two."

38

Dave hugged Kathryn when she got off the plane at three o'clock. "I'm glad to see you," he said, and reached for her bag. "I'll carry that for you."

"I can carry my own bag, don't be sexist."

"I'm not being sexist, I'm being gallant."

She handed it to him. "In that case, you can carry it."

He slung the strap over his shoulder and headed for the exit at a brisk pace. "Cherry Hills detectives say Manoff hasn't left the house. I rented a car and picked up a Denver Metro street atlas. They live in a *very* exclusive place called Cherry Hills Farm, the same place John Elway lives."

"He's a baseball player like Steve Young and Mark McGwire, right?" she asked.

"Right."

"See, I know about sports."

He snorted.

She ignored him. "Where's the car?"

"In police parking at the front of the terminal."

He dropped her bag in the trunk of the blue Tercel. "Did you contact Child Protective Services, or whatever they call it here in Colorado?"

Kathryn nodded. "Arapahoe County Health Department. Yes, I called from the in-flight phone."

He glanced over his shoulder and merged the Toyota into the heavy westbound traffic on I-70. "You saw both babies' pictures, what do you think?"

"It's hard to tell from that out-of-focus Polaroid the Alexanders gave us. We won't know for sure until we compare her DNA to the Alexanders', but they could be the same infant."

"This is gonna raise some ugly legal issues if she's been adopted by the Manoffs."

"Yep."

Kathryn poked Dave's arm and pointed. "Denver's that way."

"I didn't ask for directions, I know the way."

"Oh, I forgot, men don't ask for directions, even when they're lost."

He glared in mock indignation. "Sexist. Men don't get lost."

"Then how come you turned on I-225?"

"Because it takes us around the east side, directly to Cherry Hills Village, and avoids downtown Denver." He changed lanes to avoid a car broken down on the shoulder, exited the freeway onto Belleview Avenue West, and turned north on University Avenue.

Cherry Hills Farm was a gated community whose

cobblestone entry was lined by perfectly trimmed pyramidal evergreens. A divider planted with annuals and manicured lawns separated one-way ingress and egress lanes, and inside the beige brick walls, a man-made grassy knoll shielded the homes from the street. Cherry Hills Farm Drive meandered around the perimeter.

"Nice," Kathryn commented. "How much do you suppose these places would cost in California?"

"More than you or I will ever be able to afford."

Kathryn pulled her notebook from her purse. "The address is thirteen-fourteen Cherry Hills Farm Drive. There it is."

"Four thousand square feet, at least," Dave observed. A black wrought iron fence topped by spear tips surrounded the entire property. The two-story home was pale orange brick, with chimneys at both ends of the steep slate roof.

Upper floor windows were trimmed in white, and built into recesses created by square pillars. A brick porch lined with flower-filled terra cotta planters led to a glass-framed, arched entry door. Native shrubs and trees created an orderly but natural outdoor environment, and an intoxicating bouquet from two acres of freshly mown grass permeated the air.

The driveway curved right past the entrance and terminated at the four-car garage, above which was built an apartment. The apartment connected to the house via a patio and breezeway.

Dave idled the Toyota up the driveway and parked by a white Lexus. Before they could ring the

39

The Tercel was northbound on I-25 after leaving Arapahoe County Health Services, passing the University of Denver campus, before either Dave or Kathryn spoke.

She broke the silence. "We may have just recovered a kidnapped infant, so why do I feel like shit?"

"Because Manoff finally gets her kid, and some damn cop shows up and takes it away from her. And what's worse, it may be a helluva long time before the Alexanders bring her home. The whole goddamn situation sucks."

He glanced at Kathryn, then returned his attention to the freeway. "And that doesn't take into account Amanda, or Jane, or whatever her name is. Do you think babies that young know what's going on around them?"

"Of course. Infants recognize their primary caretakers. That's why they smile and coo when their mothers pick them up; cause-and-effect; smile and Mommy smiles back."

"How do you know that?"

"Before Emma was born I read everything I could get my hands on about child development. Infants form critical early attachments that influence the rest of their lives, from how they do in school to what kind of parents they'll become."

"Then we should feel good about taking Janey into custody and reconnecting her with her parents."

"If the reconnection happens soon enough. Babies connect to anyone who is consistently around and responds to them. That's usually the parents, simply because they're around the most, but it could be anyone. It's the connection itself that counts, not with whom it's made."

"So, if Janey doesn't connect up with her parents soon?"

"Critical areas of the brain remain undeveloped in babies that are deprived of nurturing, like those in institutional nurseries. And in shelters like the one we just left."

"We had no choice, Kate. She won't be there long."

"We don't know that. DNA testing can take weeks, and if the Manoffs fight for custody, it could be months."

"Doesn't sound like Deborah Manoff thinks her husband would fight for custody."

"He will if she insists. If he does, the baby'll be shuffled from one foster home to another, so she never bonds with anyone at all. And with the shortage of foster homes, there are a lot of unqualified people caring for kids, which could cause her permanent damage."

"She may end up being one screwed-up kid."

"For sure."

They fell silent again. When Kathryn spotted the downtown Denver skyline, she asked, "Where's our motel?"

Granz swung the car off onto Colfax Avenue. "I didn't get us motel rooms."

It was hot, and Kathryn felt tired, frustrated and irritable. "Dammit, Dave, you said you'd take care of it. How do you expect me to trust you about important things like—well, you know what—if I can't trust you to make room reservations?"

"Relax, Kate, I said I didn't get motel rooms, not that I didn't make room reservations." He turned a corner and pulled to the curb. "We're staying here, at the Brown Palace Hotel."

Built in 1892 as an expression of Victorian architecture in the Italian Renaissance style, the Brown Palace's exterior consisted of Colorado red granite and Arizona sandstone. Wedge-shaped to fit the southwest corner of Broadway Avenue and Seventeenth Street, it occupied a substantial portion of that entire city block.

Beige awnings overhung the sidewalks around the hotel, at one point sheltering the elegant main entrance. On one side of the doors, which were attended by two uniformed doormen, was a carved likeness of builder Henry C. Brown, on the other his carved initials. Between the windows of the seventh floor, carved images of native wild animals adorned the sandstone.

"It's too expensive," she protested.

He pulled to the valet station, shut off the engine, and turned to face her, propping his right leg on the console and resting his arm on the seat back. "My treat. I knew today would be hard, especially for you."

She put her hand on his arm. "Thank you. I'm sorry for being a bitch."

"It's okay."

The doorman opened the car door and helped them out, then removed the bags from the trunk, summoned a valet, and escorted them to the door. The lobby was lined with Mexican onyx.

Kathryn gazed upward past tiered cast iron balconies, to the 2,800 square-foot stained glass ceiling, six stories above the lobby floor.

"This is lovely," she commented.

"I thought something special might cheer us up. Would you like a glass of wine?"

"I want to call the Alexanders first, then take a quick shower."

Dave drank part of a beer and watched the Cardinals–Astros baseball game in the hotel's Ship Tavern. When Kathryn joined him, her hair was still damp, and she had changed into a pair of black slacks and a white, open-neck blouse with no bra. Dave noticed, through the semi-sheer blouse, that she was cold. He picked up her hand and interwove their fingers. She ordered a glass of Colorado Riesling.

"Did you reach the Alexanders?" he asked.

"I spoke with Gayle, Garrett wasn't home. I told her we won't know anything for sure until DNA tests are completed, and told her they should have their blood tested as soon as possible."

"And?"

"Maybe it's my imagination, but she almost sounded disappointed. She said she'd talk it over with Garrett and let us know."

"Let us know what? All they gotta do is get their damn blood tested. What the hell's up with them?"

Kathryn shrugged her shoulders. "I don't understand it, either, but they don't seem very interested in bringing her home. Maybe Janey, or Amanda, would be better off with the Manoffs."

"Gary Manoff doesn't want her, either."

"I know. How could a tiny, innocent baby be so awful that no one wants her, just because of a damned birthmark?"

"I don't know, Kate."

"Would you want her, Dave?"

He stared at her. "I honestly don't know."

Kate sighed and sipped at her wine, then set it down and asked, "How do you plan to handle Ledbetter?"

"As soon as possible, before Gary Manoff contacts him. Give me your return airline ticket."

Kathryn pulled an envelope from her purse and slid it to him.

"After dinner," he said, "I'll exchange our tickets for an early morning flight to San Francisco."

They sat without talking for several minutes, but

continued holding hands, oblivious to the luxurious dark, polished wood warmth and elegance of the lounge, whose walls were decorated with exquisitely crafted model clipper ships.

"Are you hungry?" Dave finally asked.

"No."

He stood and held out his hand. "Neither of us has eaten all day."

She took his hand. "I don't feel like eating."

"Would you like to take a walk through downtown? Larimer Square is pretty at night."

"No."

"Do you want to go through the shops in the lobby?"

"I don't think so."

"What would you like to do?"

"Go to your room. I don't want to sleep by myself tonight."

40

"Is your affidavit almost finished?" Mackay asked.

"Yep." Granz pointed at two handwritten sheets of paper on the seat-back tray, drained his coffee cup, and handed it to the flight attendant.

Mackay dragged her laptop from under the seat, turned it on and started Wordperfect, called up a pre-formatted search warrant form and started filling in the blanks, then she punched the number of the Santa Rita County Communications Center into the in-flight phone.

"Comm Center." The female dispatcher sounded as if she were at the far end of a hollow tunnel.

"This is District Attorney Mackay. Who's the on-call judge?"

"One moment, Ms. Mackay." The line was quiet for a moment, then the dispatcher said, "Judge Tucker is on call. She left her home phone number. Do you need it?"

"No, I have it, but would you phone her and tell

her that I'll be calling within the next few minutes to get a telephonic search warrant?"

"Anything else?"

"No. Thanks."

Mackay handed Granz a slip of paper. "Set up a three-way call while I finish the warrant."

"Tucker? Good, we won't need to bring another judge up to speed on the kidnapping." Granz attached the suction-cup pickup unit of his minicassette recorder to the phone, tested it, then punched in Tucker's number. He nodded and Mackay placed the phone to her ear.

"Judge Tucker." She yawned audibly.

"Good morning, this is Kathryn Mackay."

"Six o'clock is awfully early for a Sunday morning, Kathryn. This had better be important."

Mackay smiled. "I believe we have located Jane Alexander. We need a search warrant."

"To search what?"

"The office of a San Francisco attorney who placed Jane in an adoptive home in Colorado."

"You'll need a Special Master."

"A Special Master may not be required to search an attorney's office if he is suspected of criminal activity."

"I've read the Blasquez ruling, Kathryn. What criminal activity is this attorney suspected of?"

"Kidnapping for ransom and child abduction."

"You may run into work product and privileged documents. I'm going to have a Special Master meet you so you don't taint your investigation. Now, who's your affiant?"

"Lieutenant Granz."

"Are you on the line, Lieutenant?" she asked.

"Yes," Granz replied.

"All right. Remember that each time we speak, we must identify ourselves for the recording. Go ahead, Kathryn."

Mackay indicated for Granz to start the recorder, than announced, "The recorder is on. This is District Attorney Kathryn Mackay. Will the other parties introduce themselves, please."

"Superior Court Judge Jemima Tucker."

"Sheriff's Lieutenant David Granz."

"Your Honor, please swear the affiant," Mackay requested.

After Granz was sworn, Mackay said, "Mackay. Lieutenant Granz, please read the duplicate original warrant."

"Granz. 'Duplicate original, State of California, County of Santa Rita search warrant. The People of the State of California to any sheriff, constable, marshal, or police officer in the County of Santa Rita; there is probable cause to believe that the property or person described herein may be lawfully seizable pursuant to Penal Code Section one-five-two-four in that it tends to show that a felony has been committed.

" 'You are therefore commanded to search the business premises of Bernard Ledbetter, Attorney-at-Law, at twenty-two–fifteen Van Ness Avenue, Suite six-fifteen, San Francisco; including all rooms, storage units, file cabinets, desks, trash containers and other parts therein

" 'for the following property: utility bills, rent receipts, letters, addressed envelopes, keys, bank statements, deposit receipts, wire transfer receipts for deposits and withdrawals, canceled checks, cash receipts and disbursements journals, and client trust records dated subsequent to May first this year, and bring it forthwith before this court.' "

"Mackay. Lieutenant Granz, relate your assignment, background, and probable cause for the warrant."

The judge interrupted. "Skip it, the Court is familiar with affiant's professional qualifications. Just relate the probable cause."

"Granz. On June three of this year, six-week-old female infant Jane Alexander was kidnapped from her Santa Rita home. Ransom was demanded of her parents and complied with, but the baby was not returned. I supervised the investigation and am familiar with the victim's physical appearance, which includes a recognizable port-wine stain on the chest, from the collarbone to just above the navel.

"DA Mackay informed me that she had spoken by phone with a Deborah Manoff, who claimed she may have the infant near Denver, Colorado. I went with Mackay to the Manoff home in Cherry Hills Farm, where I contacted Deborah Manoff, who had in her custody a female infant who appeared to be the same age and physical appearance as Jane Alexander, including the distinctive port-wine stain.

"Manoff stated she and her husband paid Bernard Ledbetter to obtain an infant for adoption, and that the infant arrived on June eleven, three days subsequent to Jane Alexander's abduction in Santa Rita. I took the baby into protective custody and turned her over to the Arapahoe County Health Department pending positive identification."

"This is Mackay. Is Her Honor satisfied that probable cause for the warrant has been shown?"

"Yes."

"Does Her Honor authorize Lieutenant Granz to sign her name to the duplicate original warrant?"

"Yes."

Mackay directed and described the remaining formalities, including Granz's signing the warrant with Tucker's name, then terminated the recording.

"Thanks, Judge," Mackay said.

"Kathryn, is Ledbetter involved in the abduction of all those other babies, too?"

"I hope so, Jimmy," Mackay answered, using the judge's nickname known only to a few close friends and trusted colleagues. "Because if he isn't, we have no clue who is, or where to find them."

41

Downtown San Francisco was typically foggy and cold, with light Sunday morning traffic.

Granz parked the Avis Saturn in a red zone at 2215 Van Ness Avenue, behind a black-and-white patrol car. In front of the police car, a short, neatly but casually dressed Asian man exited a beige Ford and walked back to greet them.

"I'm James Cheng," he said, "with Cheng, Waysmith and McCray, a civil litigation firm here in San Francisco. I was assigned as Special Master at the request of Judge Tucker. May I see the search warrant, please."

Two uniformed police officers climbed out of the patrol car and introduced themselves as Officers Harold Raines and Elizabeth Walker. Raines was in his late forties, tall and heavy; Walker was a short, thin young woman with a pockmarked face.

"We're just here as backup, you gotta do the

search yerselves," Raines stated bluntly, making a production of checking his wristwatch.

Walker made eye contact with Granz. "Should we roust the custodian?"

"Yeah, thanks," Granz replied.

Raines leaned on the bell until a tall, skinny, blond-haired kid appeared carrying a criminal law textbook with his index finger stuck in to mark the page. Walker motioned for him to unlock the door.

"What's your name?" Raines asked.

"Ron Gross."

"You a lawyer?"

He shook his head. "First-year law at Golden Gate."

"Figures." Raines pointed generally toward Granz, Mackay and Cheng. "They've got a warrant to search . . ." He turned to Granz. "What's the suite number?"

"Six-fifteen."

Cheng handed the warrant to Gross, who inspected it, looked up, and handed it back. "I guess it looks okay."

Raines snorted. "Get the key, Clarence Darrow, and don't take all day. I got tickets to an A's game and I wanna be there early for the tailgate party."

Gross returned with a key ring, which Raines grabbed and passed to Walker. "I'll watch the lobby," he volunteered.

In the elevator, Walker told Granz and Mackay, "Don't mind my partner. He's just an asshole."

"No need to apologize for him," Mackay assured her.

Granz rapped on the outer door to suite 615,

whose frosted glass door bore gold leaf lettering that read, BERNARD L. LEDBETTER, ESQ. ATTORNEY AT LAW ADOPTIVE LAW.

When no one answered, he dismissed Gross, who gratefully hurried to the elevator and disappeared without looking back, then unlocked the door and swung it open and stepped inside.

"Police officers," he announced in a loud voice. "We have a search warrant." There was no response, so he flipped the switch beside the door. Cheng followed.

"Jesus, a little ostentatious, don't you think?" he commented.

The reception room contained two huge black, deeply cushioned leather chairs and a translucent white, free-form Oriental alabaster coffee table. Two abstract oil paintings in white frames hung on adjacent walls, and an obsidian sculpture sat on a white marble pedestal. The white carpeting was deep and plush.

A chest-high, white marble partition and swinging gate separated the reception area from a secretarial station fitted with a built-in black-and-white marble desktop, chrome chair, a futuristic Compaq mini-tower computer, and built-in file cabinets.

Ledbetter's office was similarly furnished, with several sculptures mounted on marble stands around the perimeter. Behind the desk, a two-foot high crystal sculpture on a black Grecian pedestal suggested, rather than depicted, the form of a newborn infant.

Granz motioned for the cop to remain in the reception area, then with Cheng, methodically searched for hidden doorways and secreted safes or other storage devices.

Mackay observed from a distance. Cheng watched Granz closely, but didn't assist with the search. Granz found the desk locked, pulled a key ring from his pocket, and unfolded the arms of a SWISS-TECH mini-multitool. He pried the center and top left drawers open and rummaged through various office and personal items, then did the same with the remaining drawers. Then with a set of keys he found in the desk, he tossed the file cabinets.

"Not a goddamn thing," he said. He sat in Ledbetter's chair and looked around. "Notice anything about his office?"

"Other than it cost a fortune to furnish, no," Mackay answered. "Why?"

"He doesn't have his own computer."

"Most attorneys don't. So what?"

"So, maybe his secretary's involved and she maintains the financial records on her computer. Let's find out."

Granz sat at the secretary desk and flipped on the Compaq while Mackay and Cheng watched over his shoulder. It booted up without password protection, and opened to the Windows98 start menu.

"Let's see what's on here," he mused. He clicked on "Start," then "Programs."

He rolled the mouse, scrolling the cursor slowly along the drop-down menu. "Nothing but standard Windows utilities and Microsoft Office. Let's check out MS-Money."

He opened Microsoft Money and clicked on "files," then "open."

"Shit, no data files are set up. It looks like Ledbetter keeps his financial records the old-fashioned way."

"Where?" Mackay asked. "They weren't in his desk or the file cabinets. Maybe he keeps them at home."

"I doubt it. He'd need to carry them back and forth every day."

"Safe deposit box?"

"Same problem, and even if he started out cautious, after a while he'd get complacent. They're here in the office someplace."

He sat at Ledbetter's desk again, thought momentarily, then opened the lower left drawer. He located a ruler, measured the drawer's depth, then tapped it all around the inside.

"Pay dirt," he said.

He removed the drawer and turned it upside down on the floor. "False bottom," he told them, then pried off the bottom panel with his Swisstool and lifted out a dark brown accordion folder marked PAID BILLS, with slots labeled JANUARY to DECEMBER. "There they are."

He flipped through them, and pulled one out, which he showed to Cheng first, then Mackay.

"Pac Bell telephone bill for May of this year." Within a couple of minutes, he had assembled, inventoried, tagged and secured several invoices, rent receipts and other items in Ledbetter's name, and sealed them in an evidence bag.

Beside the accordion file, Granz found a six-ring commercial checkbook marked, CLIENT TRUST #2 and opened it on the desk. The right side contained about a hundred blank green checks imprinted with Ledbetter's name and address. A hundred or so stubs, which remained after their matching checks had been written and torn out, were on the left.

"This guy should have been a damn bookkeeper, look how neat his checkbook is."

"The warrant limits your search to the period after May first," Cheng reminded him.

"I know." He flipped to May, ran his forefinger down the page, and stopped at a handwritten entry in the Deposits section of the top stub. "Look."

The deposit notation read, "Wire-5/3/GM/ $50,000." Four sheets of stubs later, another deposit notation said, "6/10/Wire/GM/$50,000."

Flipping back to May 1, he noted other wire deposits and withdrawals, all in large, round amounts. On June 9, two wire transfers out were recorded; $10,000 to "MF," and $15,000 to "B."

"The bank statement will disclose the account numbers on the other end of those wire transfers. I bet the two fifty-thou deposits will trace to the Manoffs, and the ten grand transfer to Fredericks."

"Payment for Jane Alexander?"

"That'd be my guess."

"Who's 'B'?"

"Don't know yet."

He leaned over, stuck his hand under the desk, fished around, and released the lower right drawer.

"Another false bottom." He removed a bundle of brown envelopes. "Bank statements—all bundled up and reconciled." Before Cheng could check them, the telephone rang on Ledbetter's desk.

"Kate, why don't you pick it up at the secretary's desk," he suggested.

She picked up. "Good morning, law office of Bernard Ledbetter."

"Is Bernard in?" a man's voice asked.

"No, he isn't, may I help you?"

"I just spoke to his housekeeper a few minutes ago. She said he was on his way to the office. Take down my name and number and have him return my call the instant he arrives."

Mackay wrote down the information, then the line disconnected and she stared at the handset before gingerly replacing it on the receiver.

"Who was that?" Granz asked.

"Gary Manoff."

42

"Who the fuck are you?" Bernard Ledbetter stopped short when he spotted Mackay beside the secretary's desk. He wore maroon polyester trousers and a Hawaiian floral shirt. Rotund, bald and beet-faced, his jowls bounced like a bantam rooster's wattles as he glanced around quickly.

Mackay guessed his age at fifty, but figured she could be off by fifteen years either way. "Are you Bernard Ledbetter?" she asked.

He regained his composure and closed the entry door. "Who wants to know?"

James Cheng heard the door open and close, and walked into the reception area. "I do," Cheng told him, then handed Ledbetter the warrant.

Ledbetter read it. "This is bullshit! You can't search my office without a Special Master, so get the fuck out."

Cheng presented his identification and California State Bar card. "I am the Special Master."

Ledbetter glared, then stalked into his private office, followed by Cheng and Mackay.

Granz was seated at the desk. He stood and handed a piece of paper to Ledbetter. "Here's the return for the property we seized."

Ledbetter inspected the inventory. "Bank statements and check stubs for the past two months? Whatever you dumb shits are looking for, you won't find it. I'm calling my lawyer."

Granz motioned for Mackay to join him in the reception area. "I need to get him to the SFPD and interrogate him. He's our only link to the babies."

"Hey!" Ledbetter was watching Granz and Mackay with his hand over the telephone mouthpiece. When they looked his direction, he said, "My attorney says if you've finished, either arrest me or get the hell out. Am I under arrest?"

"Are you willing to talk to us?" Granz asked.

Ledbetter spoke into the phone and listened. "My attorney says I don't have anything to say."

Granz turned to Mackay. "Do we have enough to take him into custody?"

She shook her head. "No."

Ledbetter spoke into the phone again, listened, then said, "Okay, okay, I'll wait, but don't be too long," and hung up.

"I'm invoking my Miranda rights, in case you don't understand English," he told Mackay and Granz. "And as soon as you leave, my attorney and I are going to draw up papers to sue all your asses."

43

"What now?" He muted the television and grabbed the phone.

"The police just searched Ledbetter's office. They seized his bank statements and financial records."

"How do you know?"

"He called me while they were there, and asked what to do."

"What'd you tell 'im?"

"To keep his mouth shut, and wait at his office for me to contact him. Let me know as soon as you get there. You know what to do."

"Fuckin'-A."

After swinging into a Santa Clara Mini Mart for smokes, he drove to San Francisco, parked across the street from 2215 Van Ness Avenue, and punched a local number into his cell phone.

"I'm here. Gimme fifteen minutes, then send the cocksucker down."

"Watch your language," she admonished.

"Fuck off." He laughed and hung up, then crossed the

street and stuck a knife into the left front tire of Ledbetter's white Lincoln and returned to his car.

He watched Ledbetter approach the parking lot, stop, step back to inspect his car, then spot the flat tire.

Ledbetter opened the trunk, fumbled around to locate the jack, and raised the front of the car off the ground.

When the lawyer knelt at the tire to start removing lug bolts, he strode briskly across Van Ness Avenue and stopped momentarily at the parking lot entrance to retrieve a ten-inch, black handled Kershaw hunting knife from a sheath inside the rear waistband of his trousers.

Silently, cigarette dangling from his lips, he approached Ledbetter from behind and in one swift movement, grabbed Ledbetter's forehead, yanked his head backward, looked briefly into the lawyer's startled eyes, and drew the Kershaw across the throat.

Ledbetter gurgled, twitched and tried to turn his head, but the severed neck muscles couldn't respond. He collapsed forward with his face on top of the tire, which was still mounted on the car. In great, pulsing spurts from two severed jugulars, blood gushed over the tire and ran down the sides to lap around the jack base in a steaming red puddle. The lug wrench clattered to the pavement.

He checked the razor-sharp blade of the Kershaw, found it clean, and shoved it back into the sheath. He waited for a break in traffic, then re-crossed Van Ness Avenue and climbed into his car.

He lighted a fresh Marlboro, coughed, spat a bloody yellow, stringy glob of phlegm out the window, then started the big V-8 engine and aimed the black Suburban south toward I-280, San Jose.

44

"Hey Mom, wake up." Emma scooped up a handful of warm sand and dribbled it on her mother's back, then giggled.

Kathryn opened her eyes and ran a hand across her shoulder, but the sand stuck to the sunscreen. "Em! Why did you do that?"

" 'Cause you were asleep and I'm hungry."

"I wasn't sleeping, I was resting my eyelids."

"Uh-uh, you were sleeping. Let's race our bikes up the hill. If I beat you to Sophie's, you have to buy me a quesadilla and Coke for dinner, and ice cream at Baskin-Robbins for dessert."

"What if *I* win?"

"You have to buy me a quesadilla and ice cream."

"Oh, that's a good deal."

Kathryn sat up, clasped her arms around her legs, rested her chin on her knees and gazed at the placid azure water lapping gently against the old cement ship and pier before rolling on shore. She had called

Emma from her cell phone while driving back from San Francisco and suggested they spend the rest of the day at the beach. When she got home, Emma had gathered their beach gear and was in her swimsuit.

She couldn't remember the last time she and Em had bicycled to South Cliffs Beach State Park and spent the day doing nothing, and didn't want the day to end, but reluctantly stood and shook the sand out of their beach blanket then gave it to her daughter. "Rub the sand off my back, sweetie, please."

Emma rubbed vigorously, but the dislodged sand fell inside the back of Kathryn's swimsuit and into her shorts. "Why don't we go to the store and buy something so I can cook a special Sunday dinner at home?"

Emma rolled her eyes. "All you know how to cook is lasagna, and I'm tired of that. Let's have quesadillas."

"Oh, all right, but let's not race, I feel too lazy, and you'd win anyway."

"Y-a-a-y," Emma screamed, and raced across the beach, unlocked her bike and started up the steep trail. By the time Kathryn bungeed the beach blanket and bag on her own bike and reached the top of the hill, Emma was waiting in the shade of an old cypress tree. Together, they pedaled the final mile to Sophie's Taqueria in South Cliffs Village and ordered quesadillas. Kathryn had eaten half a dozen chips with guacamole when her pager beeped.

"Aw, Mom, don't answer it," Emma pleaded. "You've been gone almost a week."

"You know I have to, honey. I'll be quick. Eat some chips and guacamole."

"I hate guacamole."

"No you don't, you've always liked it before."

"Well, I hate it today." Emma dipped a huge chip in the salsa and popped it into her mouth defiantly, but her mother was frowning at the pager and didn't notice her lapse in manners, so she did it again.

Kathryn recognized the familiar number on the pager display, and dialed.

"Dave? Kate."

"Hi, Kate," Dave greeted her. "I've got some news. Somebody whacked out Bernard Ledbetter. The custodian discovered the body in the parking lot not long after we left with his throat slit ear-to-ear. SFPD says the perp probably punctured a tire on his car, then cut his throat while he was bent over changing the flat. A professional looking job."

Kathryn sighed. "Damn."

"We still have the bank records. Not much, but it's the same as we had before someone canceled his ticket. I'll have Escalante contact the bank first thing tomorrow morning."

"Keep me posted."

"You've got it." He paused but didn't hang up.

"Was there something more?" Kathryn asked.

"I . . . would it be all right if I spoke to Emma for a minute?" he asked.

"Dave, I don't think—"

Emma's head popped up and she reached for the phone. "I want to talk to Dave before you hang up, Mom."

"Just for a minute," Kathryn said.

"Dave, guess where we went today," Emma said excitedly.

Kathryn watched as Emma listened to Dave's question, then answered, "No, I hate the ballet. We went to the beach."

Em listened again. "Yep, where the cement ship is, but Mom won't let me go out on the boat or even the pier 'cause she's afraid." She giggled. "Sharks, prob'ly. I'll ask." She covered the phone and looked at Kathryn. "Mom, Dave wants to know if he can take me to the cement boat next weekend and walk all the way out to the end, then have burritos and Cokes."

"I don't know if—"

"Dave needs to talk with me about something important."

"Oh, all right."

When Emma finished chatting, Kathryn took the phone back. "That was dirty pool," she told him, but she was smiling.

"A guy needs all the leverage he can get," he laughed, then said seriously, "Don't worry, babe, I won't say anything that would put pressure on you."

"What *do* you want to do?" she teased.

"Be so good to you that you realize I'm too good to let go of."

She disconnected and dropped the cell phone in her bag. "Maybe I already do," she mumbled.

"What, Mom?"

"Nothing, honey. Finish your quesadilla."

* * *

The ringing telephone was audible from the front landing, through the door of their condo. Emma planted her fists on her hips and scrunched her face in mock indignation, and Kathryn shrugged apologetically before dashing to the kitchen.

"Hello."

A distant, hollow buzz partially obscured the man's voice. "Kathryn?"

"Who is this?"

"Steve Giordano, Kathryn. I called to tell you that Robert Simmons has escaped from Costa Rican custody."

"What the hell do you mean, Simmons escaped? How? and when?"

"Right after the embassy received your extradition packet asking for the death penalty. As for how, officially, he overpowered a guard while furloughed to a free medical clinic. Unofficially, he was escorted to the airport by Costa Rican officials and given a one-way ticket out of Costa Rica to avoid the diplomatic embarrassment of refusing extradition."

"Damn, I shouldn't have been so stubborn."

"I won't say I told you so, Kate. According to Costa Rica Air, he flew to Mexico City."

"Any trace of him?"

"My contacts haven't turned him up."

"Now what?"

"I'll pull a few strings, check air carriers' passenger manifests out of Mexico for that date. Maybe I can narrow the destinations down to a few possibilities. I'll let you know what I turn up."

45

"Morgan, if someone with medical training tried to resuscitate a person who wasn't breathing, would a tracheotomy be the first thing they'd try?" Mackay sat in the lone chair across from Morgan Nelson's desk in his small office at the morgue.

Nelson shook his head. "They'd try CPR first—a trach would be the last resort."

"The autopsy report on the dead infant's body from Mt. Cabrillo Park said he had two cracked ribs. Could they have resulted from an unsuccessful CPR attempt?"

"Sure. When people try to resuscitate a baby, they usually compress the chest too hard, as if they're working on another adult. Broken ribs are common in those situations."

"Would a CPR attempt leave enough saliva on the infant's mouth for DNA matching?"

"Maybe. I took several oral swabs; we could send them to a lab for testing."

She contemplated. "Go ahead. Fredericks is dead, so it won't mean diddly shit if we match it to her, but I have a feeling we'll get a match to a cigarette butt we recovered at one of the crime scenes."

"Okay. What else is on your mind?"

She leaned back in the chair. "What makes you think there's something else on my mind?"

"You never stop by my office at . . ." he checked his watch. ". . . seven-thirty on Monday morning unless I'm cutting, and you called me Morgan, not Doc."

"You know me too well. Just wanted to talk."

Nelson rocked his chair back, put his feet on the corner of his desk, crossed his ankles, and clasped his hands behind his head. "I'm all ears."

She hesitated, then looked up. "Do you remember the conversation you and I had right after Dave had that—that *affair* with Julia Soto?"

"Of course. I said that you'd find it hard to deal with Dave's betrayal."

"And you agreed that I had to break off my relationship with him."

"Yep. Has something changed?"

She nodded. "Dave and I have been talking."

"Nothing unusual about that."

"He says he learned a lot from our time apart, that he loves me and thinks we can work it out."

"What do you think?"

"I don't know."

He didn't answer.

"Dave wants to take Emma to the beach next weekend. She thinks something's going on between him and me."

"Is there?"

"I'm not sure."

"How is them going to the beach a problem?"

She checked her watch and stood up. "It's probably not, but I hate to take the risk."

"Risk for whom, Emma or you?"

"Both."

46

"I'm DA Inspector Donna Escalante."

"Rafael Suarez."

Branch manager Suarez was about 35, slim, with straight, jet-black hair and a big smile that exhibited perfect white teeth, and wore a tailored brown suit and beige shirt that accentuated his piercing brown eyes.

He invited Escalante to sit in the plush client chair, then smiled and sat behind his desk. Pacific Pescadores Community Bank was in an elegantly refurbished fish cannery above South Cliffs Beach State Park, and Escalante could see the summer crowd already setting up on the sand through his office window.

"The documents themselves are kept at our main branch," he began, "but our attorney instructed me to access the bank's central computer files and print out copies of anything covered by the warrant. What would you like to know?"

Escalante passed him two bank statements on which several transactions had been marked in yellow. "Can you tell which branch services this account?"

"San Francisco Van Ness Avenue, our headquarters."

"What about the highlighted transactions?"

"They're electronic funds transfers, what we call EFTs, into and out of the account."

He turned one of them sideways and leaned forward, brushing his forearm against Escalante's and pointed to two transactions. "These deposits came from Denver. The withdrawals went to a Northern California bank." He slid his finger across the statement. "This deposit originated at our branch as an account-to-account transfer."

"Would the account owner know about the transactions before they're posted to the account?" Escalante asked.

"Sure. The customer tells us in advance the name and account number at the other end."

"Is that information maintained in your computer?"

"No, it's kept at the servicing branch."

"In writing?"

"For debits, yes. Customers don't like us to take money out of their account without permission, but they don't care if we put money in, so deposit credits can be authorized verbally, even by phone."

"Are you saying you can't help with deposits?"

"No, but I need to log onto the central computer. It captures EFTs and trace numbers, and adds them to hard-copy transactions in our reports." He scrolled through several screens before stopping.

"You'll have to come around here and look over my shoulder," he told Escalante. When she hesitated, he smiled and added, "I don't bite, Inspector."

She could sense his presence as she scanned the computer monitor.

```
    11,12102755,DEMO,990621,1002,/
    12,4432015147,USD,098,907050,/
    25,23190126,05329915129,990504,0937,/
    X8,5CR,820,5000000,0,/
    X8,FUNDS TRANSFER SOURCE PRACCT,/
    X8,REF23190126JNE081,/
    25,CKS,1099,53752,1147,2750,/
    25,12102755,12102755,990522,0859,/
    X8,BCR,820,5000000,0,/
    X8,4432:5516,015147:112219,991818,/
    X8,FUNDS IA TRANSFER IN,/
    25,CID,821,1000000,0,12100035,/
    X8,4432011255,990523,2359,/
    X8,FUNDS TRANSFER OUT
PRACCT,991821,/
    25,CID,821,1500000,0,12100024,/
    X8,6622644320,990523,2359,/
    X8,FUNDS TRANSFER OUT
PRACCT,991822,/
    25,1149,50000,1152,2650,1158,275000,/
    25,23190126,05329915129,990607,0915,/
    X8,5CR,820,5000000,0,/
    X8,FUNDS TRANSFER SOURCE PRACCT,/
    X8,REF23190126JNE099,/
```

25,CKS,1182,54332,1183,111527,1178,/
25,CDP,250000,/
25,CID,821,1000000,0,12100035,/
X8,44320111255,/990609,2359,/
X8,FUNDS TRANSFER OUT
PRACCT,991827,/
25,CID,821,1500000,0,12100024,/
X8,6622644320,990609,2359,/
X8,FUNDS TRANSFER OUT
PRACCT,991828,/
25,CKS,1099,53752,1147,2750,/
25,CID,821,3000000,0,12100035,/
X8,44320111255,/990618,2359,/
X8,FUNDS TRANSFER OUT
PRACCT,991836,/
25,CID,821,4500000,0,12100024,/
X8,6622644320,990618,2359,/
X8,FUNDS TRANSFER OUT
PRACCT,991837,/

"Looks like gibberish," she commented.

He laughed again. "I know. This is an account activity report from May first through close of business yesterday, the dates on your warrant. It's mostly BAI code—Bank Administration Institute."

He held up a worn brochure. "This deciphers it and lists routing symbols and ABA transit numbers for every bank in the U.S."

Suarez pulled another chair beside his for Escalante.

"The American Banking Association gives all banks an ABA transit number so transactions can be routed to the bank of origin for processing," he explained. "That leaves a trail that our computers recognize, capture and record, and which we can trace."

Suarez pointed to a blank check. "The first four digits of the MICR strip at the bottom indicate a bank's federal reserve district. The next four are the bank's individual identifier, the four after that which branch services the account, and last six are the account number, which can be looked up to find out the owner's name, address, TIN and phone number."

"That's a check. What about EFTs?"

He pointed to the computer monitor. "Each line on the report contains data fields separated by commas. For example, line eleven shows PPCB's ABA transit number followed by today's date and time. Line twelve tells us the account covered by the report. USD means it's stated in American dollars. Oh-nine-eight means the next numbers are the account balance; nine thousand, seventy dollars and fifty cents. Lines that start with twenty-five and X8 are transaction lines."

Escalante referred to the code brochure, then the monitor, and pointed at a transaction line. "If I've got it right, this deposit came from account 9–9–1–5–1–2–9 at the Aurora Colorado branch of Columbine State Bank in June, at nine-fifteen A.M. It was an Automated Clearing House EFT-In, for fifty thousand dollars from a private account."

"Excellent, Inspector, you've got it," Suarez told her.

"Can you print a copy of the report for me?" she asked.

When he gave it to her, she dropped it and the code brochure in her briefcase. "May I call if I run into problems translating the rest of the report, Mr. Suarez?"

"Please call me anytime, even if you don't have a problem."

Escalante flushed and stood. "Thank you, but I'm sure it won't be necessary."

"I'm sorry to hear that," he answered.

"What do you mean?"

He rose and walked around the desk. "I'd like to see you again, if you wouldn't mind. Is that possible?"

"I . . . yes."

"Then may I call you?"

Escalante hesitated, then removed a business card from her purse and jotted something on it. "My home number is on the back."

He extended his hand, and squeezed gently until she pulled away. "It was a pleasure meeting you, Inspector Escalante."

"Donna," she corrected him.

47

Santa Rita summer mornings are typically damp, foggy and cold, but by midmorning, a bright, hot sun burned through the grimy windows of Kathryn Mackay's office at the Government Center, raising the interior temperature to an uncomfortable level. The building's central air conditioning was seldom necessary, and rarely worked when it was, so she walked to the windows which faced the park and reluctantly drew the drapes. Dust floated from the heavy material, causing her to sneeze three times in rapid succession.

"¡Salud!" Donna Escalante said, opening the door and admitting herself.

"Muchas gracias, Adelante," Mackay replied.

Escalante slid a leather client chair up close to Kathryn Mackay's desk and sat down. "I interpreted every transaction recorded in Ledbetter's account since May first," she began, "and traced the payments in and out to their source." She handed a manila folder to Mackay, and spread hers open on Mackay's desk.

"Summarize it," Mackay directed.

"I identified three electronic cash deposits for $50,000 each, two of them from a bank in Aurora, Colorado, that coincide with the payments Manoff said they made to Ledbetter to arrange the adoption. The account belongs to Gary and Deborah Manoff."

"What about the third?"

"On May twenty-second, PPCB's South Santa Rita branch initiated an inter-branch transfer to Ledbetter from a local account, but the bank manager refuses to divulge the owner's identity without a search warrant for that account."

Mackay jotted a note on a yellow legal pad. "Go on."

"Two simultaneous electronic transfers were made from Ledbetter's account on June ninth, the day after Jane Alexander was abducted. One for fifteen thousand to a CalWestern Bank in Santa Clara; one for ten-thousand bucks went into a Sierra National account in San Jose belonging to Monica Fredericks."

"Damn."

"She made an over-the-counter withdrawal the next morning and removed the entire ten grand," Escalante added.

"What about CalWestern?" Mackay asked.

"Bank records say it belongs to a man named Sam Spade. His address turns out to be a vacant lot in Los Gatos. The phone number doesn't exist, and the driver's license and Social Security numbers he provided are phony. The fifteen thousand bucks deposited on June third was withdrawn in cash, over-the-counter, when the bank opened the next morning."

"Same as Fredericks," Mackay mused.

"Thirty thousand more was credited to Fredericks' account as of midnight, Friday, June eighteenth. She was in Cleveland, so she probably planned to wire the money to herself the following Monday, but was murdered Saturday morning. Thirty thou's still in the account."

"What about Spade's account?"

"Forty-five thousand was deposited at the same time."

"And withdrawn the next morning?"

"That branch isn't open Saturdays, besides, I think Spade was in Cleveland murdering Fredericks, probably didn't get back to the Bay Area until late that afternoon or the next morning. The money's still there."

"What makes you think he returned to the Bay Area?"

"Ledbetter. Fredericks and Spade were partners," Escalante speculated. "Their bank accounts were opened at the same time, the deposit timing is identical, withdrawals, too; in one day, out the next."

"The only difference is the amounts," Mackay observed. "Fredericks got ten grand for each baby, Spade got fifteen. He must've been the boss?"

"One of the bosses, at least. And he was a lot smarter than Fredericks. He opened the account under a fake name and ID numbers. There's no way he can be traced through that bank account. She wasn't bright enough to cover her tracks."

"Or, she was too inexperienced."

"Maybe. We need to research Ledbetter's account activity prior to May first."

"Looking for what?"

"The Manoffs made two payments of fifty thousand each to obtain their baby; the first on May fourth was a search fee, the second on June seventh was the day before they got Amanda. My guess is that the May twenty-second fifty-thousand dollar deposit was final payment for an abduction that had already happened. If so, I'll find the related search fee in March or April."

"And if you're right," Mackay interjected, "you'll find corresponding ten and fifteen-thousand dollar EFTs to Fredericks and Spade immediately after."

Escalante nodded. "I laid out time lines, plotted abductions on one, deposits into Ledbetter's accounts on the second, transfers out of his account on the third, and deposits into Fredericks' and Spade's accounts on the fourth. They match the pattern."

Mackay shook her head. "Hard to believe. Babies being bought and sold like commodities."

"Stolen and very expensive commodities, at that," Escalante answered. "If I'm right, we'll find the fifty-thousand dollar down payments for the Sweet, Flowers and Flynt infants, too. They were all snatched within a two-day period, and there are lump sum payments to Fredericks and Spade of thirty and forty-five thousand not long after."

"Get search warrants for Ledbetter's earlier bank records, along with Fredericks' and Spade's."

"Will do. Anything else?"

"Damn right," Mackay told her. "The PPCB account from which the May twenty inter-branch deposit to Ledbetter's account was taken. Whoever it belongs to bought a family."

48

"Afternoon, Kate. Got a minute?"

Mackay looked up from the stack of papers on her desk. "Sure, Dave, sit down."

"Just got a call from Lamarr in Cleveland. They found where the shooter was when he killed Fredericks—an office building roof a couple of blocks from the Justice Tower. They think he killed the security guard, then waited on the roof for his chance."

"What makes them think so?"

"He left behind a portable Casio color TV, still tuned to the Turner Classic Movie Channel, and a pile of cigarette butts."

"What brand?"

"Marlboro."

The large magnetic sign on each door advertised, SANTA RITA MOBILE AUTO DETAILING—***if dirt can find your car, so can we.***

He idled the black Suburban slowly through the rows of

parked cars, checking each one carefully, then spotted a red BMW and stopped at its rear bumper.

He pulled a pack of Marlboros from over the visor, stuck one between his lips and lit up, but he hadn't enjoyed a smoke since putting the Halloween teeth and mustache on before leaving San Jose.

After adjusting the horn-rim glasses, which distorted his vision despite the lenses being plain glass, he grabbed a plastic bucket, spray bottles of Quicksilver wheel cleaner and Maguires Mirror Glaze Final Inspection, a handful of rags and a screwdriver. He pulled the Giants cap down firmly over the blond ponytail wig and headphones, then strolled over to the Beemer.

The first step was to take the Beemer's front and rear license plates off. When that was done, he sprayed cleaner on all four polished aluminum wheels and buffed them to a brilliant shine then, moving in time with the oldies music on KOCN, he started waxing the paint.

"Hey!"

He looked up to see a green-and-white sheriff's patrol unit behind his Suburban. A young deputy stuck his head out the window and motioned for him to remove the headphone.

"Jesus, are you deaf?" the deputy asked.

He turned off the radio and approached the car; propped his elbow on the roof, and leaned over. "Naw, man, I was lis'nin' to the radio. Helps pass the time, fuckin' job gets boring, ya know?"

"Tell me about it," the deputy replied. "You oughta try driving around in a cop car for ten hours a day and can't even smoke in it. What are you doing, anyway?"

He pointed at the sign on his truck. "Detailin' that BMW. Owner's too lazy to do it herself. I don't give a rat's ass, dumb broad pays me seventy-five bucks for an hour's work. My luck, though, it's gotta be the hottest day of the year. Sweat's already runnin' down my back like a river."

"Seventy-five bucks, huh? You give law enforcement discounts?"

"Damn straight." He pulled half a dozen business cards from his wallet. "Pass these around. Tell your buddies I'll do their cars for fifty. While they work. You pull it in dirty an' when yer shift's over it'll look like new."

The deputy stuffed the cards in his uniform shirt pocket, flipping his badge and name tag so it could be read from outside the car. "Fifty bucks? That's a little steep."

He grinned. "Tell ya what, Deputy Roberts, I'll make it thirty-five for you. For the other guys it's forty-five, but you gotta keep it between me 'n' you. I got a business reputation to consider."

"Thanks, I'll give you a call."

"Do that, you dumb asshole," he said as the green-and-white pulled away. "Now where's that fuckin' Explorer?"

49

"This is a mistake of some kind." Mackay picked up the report and flipped it over, as if the back side might contain different results, or an explanation for the anomaly, then dropped it on her desk. "Cellmark's DNA report says Amanda Manoff isn't Jane Alexander."

"I called as soon as they faxed me the report, but you were gone."

"I went shopping on my lunch hour. Have you contacted the Alexanders?"

"No, I wanted to talk to you first. If Garrett and Gayle Alexander aren't the parents, we're back where we started and Jane Alexander's still missing."

"Well, at least Amanda can go back home to the Manoffs," Mackay responded. "Maybe it's true that every silver lining has a cloud."

Granz shook his head. "The saying goes, 'every cloud has a silver lining,' Kate, not the other way around. But, in this case, you might have stated it correctly, because if Gary Manoff won't take Amanda back, she'll stay in foster homes forever. There really will be a cloud behind that silver lining and it'll be our fault for taking her into protective custody. We screwed up."

"What else could we have done?"

He shrugged. "I don't know, but we've got to tell the Alexanders their baby's still missing. How do you think they'll react?"

"Based on their previous behavior," Mackay told him, "I'm not sure they'll give a damn."

Kathryn had just popped a butterscotch candy into her mouth when her pager beeped. She fumbled through her purse and checked the page; a number she didn't recognize, followed by 9–1–1.

She punched the number into her phone and when it picked up, she said, "Mackay."

"Do you know who I am?" The deep, scratchy voice sent a chill up her spine. She spat the candy into the wastebasket.

"Yes, I've been waiting for you to call."

"I want to make a deal."

"What kind of deal?"

"Unfreeze my bank account long enough for me to make a withdrawal."

"In exchange for what?"

"No one getting hurt."

Mackay thought about it briefly. Monica Fredericks. Bernard Ledbetter. Aaron Mitchum. All dead.

"Deliver Jane Alexander safe, or forget it."

He coughed, then she heard a phone booth door open and him spitting. The door slammed shut and a Zippo lighter flicked open. He drew in a deep breath and expelled it slowly.

"You'll never catch me," he declared.

"Then why do you care if I keep trying?"

"It's a pain in the ass. And I need my money."

"You walked away from McDonald's with two million bucks in ransom."

"There are big expenses in this business. I'll tell you where to find the kid after I get the money."

"That's what you said last time."

"Somethin' came up."

Mackay contemplated. "No information, no deal."

He dragged on the cigarette and exhaled. "Shit. The Alexander kid's in Colorado with some fuckin' lawyer and his wife."

Mackay sat up in her chair. "How do you know?"

"I delivered her."

"I'm listening."

"Place called Cherry Hills. Don't remember the name or address, but you oughta be able to find 'em, no problem."

Mackay fingered Cellmark's DNA report and frowned. "You're sure?"

"What th' fuck did I say? Sure I'm sure."

"What about the others?"

"What others?"

"The other infants you kidnapped."

"Don't jack me around, Mackay, you traded the money for the Alexander kid. I gave you the kid, now keep your enda the goddamn deal."

"Give me the others and I'll let you have your money. Otherwise, forget it."

"I shoulda killed you when I had the chance."

"Yeah, but you didn't."

"I will."

"Kiss my ass."

The other end of the line went silent for several seconds, then he said, "I figured you'd think yer a pretty tough cunt, so I won't whack yer ass, after all. I got a better idea. Walk to your window."

She complied.

"I'm going to count backwards from fifteen. When I get to zero, duck. Fifteen, fourteen, . . . two, one."

A gigantic fireball flared in the employee parking lot below her office window, a spilt second before she heard the blast. When she looked out, she saw pieces of debris in the shape of car parts floating through the air, and a column of ugly black smoke rising into the clear sky.

"That was your boyfriend Granz' Ford Explorer. I'll give you a few hours to calm down, then call back. If you don't unfreeze my bank account, the next bomb'll take a bunch of people up with it."

50

"Let's get started." Granz glanced around the sheriff's conference room at District Attorney Mackay, DA Inspector Escalante, DA Chief of Inspectors James Fields and DOJ criminalist Roselba Menendez.

"At two-eighteen this afternoon," Granz began, "a bomb exploded in the government center parking lot. It completely destroyed one car—my goddamn new Ford Explorer—and heavily damaged several others."

"What kind of device?" Fields asked.

Granz looked at Menendez. "Our bomb experts tentatively conclude it was probably a TupperWare container filled with commercial fertilizer and diesel fuel," she told them.

Escalante leaned forward with her elbows on the conference table. "TupperWare?"

Menendez nodded. "Bombs need to be tightly encased so the fuel can combust and build up pressure after it's ignited. TupperWare is perfect because it seals very tight and requires a lot of force to remove the lid. Not an uncommon technique."

"How was it detonated?" Fields inquired.

"A model rocket fuse. Simple but effective. By itself, this device would have demolished the car it was planted under, but it was duct-taped to a five gallon propane bottle."

"Jesus," Mackay commented. "Like the tanks on travel trailers?"

"And gas barbecues," Menendez confirmed. "It produced most of the power, but the surrounding cars absorbed most of the bomb's energy. That, plus the fact that most county employees were inside during the middle of the afternoon, avoided a lot of people being killed or injured."

"We think the bomber intentionally avoided killing anyone," Granz interjected.

"A warning?" Escalante asked.

He nodded. "Absolutely."

"To whom?"

"Me," Mackay answered.

"Until we catch the sonofabitch," Granz told them, "we've got to set up tight security around the Government Center. Public Works is erecting barricades at all parking lot entrances, and uniformed deputies are inspecting every vehicle that enters."

"What about the buildings?"

"We're installing metal detectors at Government Center and courts buildings doors. I posted uniformed and plainclothes patrols throughout the buildings' interiors, the grounds, and the parking lot.

"One more thing." Granz paused. "A sheriff's patrol deputy FIed a weird looking guy in the parking lot a few minutes before the device went off."

"The deputy filled out a Field Interrogation card?" Fields asked.

"Yeah, but he didn't run the license plates through DMV at the time. I did that myself. The guy was driving a black Suburban rigged like a mobile car detailer. I put out an APB on the Suburban."

"What about the plates?" Escalante asked.

"Stolen."

"From where?"

"Kathryn Mackay's BMW."

51

A gigantic mushroom cloud billowed skyward from the Government Center parking lot. The blast sucked a green-and-white sheriff's car up into the vortex, hurled it out over the top rim, and dropped it. The car crashed into the roof of a yellow school bus filled with children, and exploded, igniting the bus and strewing dozens of tiny mangled arms, legs and torsos in ignominious heaps over a two-block area.

Remnants of the target car, Dave Granz' new red Mercedes Benz ML-320 SUV rained from the sky in hundreds of charred pieces. One landed at Kathryn Mackay's feet. She picked it up, but dropped it in horror when she found Granz' severed head inside. It looked at her with dead, but disapproving eyes.

"Why didn't you back off when the Marlboro Man called?" the head asked. "He warned you what would happen, but you were too stubborn. Now, everyone's dead and it's your fault."

"Dave! Wait! You—"

She never finished her sentence, because the angry mob of limbless, sightless corpses pressed closer and closer. They stoned her and blood dripped from her open wounds.

"Mackay the Murderer," they chanted.

"NO!!!" Kathryn sat straight up in bed, eyes wide open. "NO!!!"

She checked the clock beside her bed. Five-fifteen A.M. She picked up the phone and punched in Dave Granz' home number.

"We've got to catch him," Kathryn stated, "and we don't have much time."

Dave closed her office door and handed her a Starbucks cup with a brown thermal sleeve, then sat in one of her leather chairs. "I know."

"He threatened to kill you."

He set his coffee cup on the desk and leaned forward. "It was just a dream, Kate. I told you last night I'm not scared for myself, and even if I were, I couldn't let it affect the investigation. Neither can you, it goes with the territory."

"The dream was so real."

"But it was still just your imagination. I want the sonofabitch as much as you."

She frowned. "What I can't figure out is why he needs us to unfreeze his bank account. His share of the Alexander ransom has to amount to ten times what's in his bank account. Why doesn't he just blow it off?"

"He would if he had it, so I figure he must've turned it over to someone else, maybe Ledbetter, until they could be sure the bills weren't marked. Or, maybe he sent it off-shore to be laundered and sent back at forty or fifty cents on the dollar. Except the transactions weren't completed before the shit hit the fan and it's too late. He needs the money in that account, so I say let's unfreeze it so he can get his cash and be on his way."

"Won't he just open a new account at another bank and have the money wire transferred to it as soon as we unfreeze it? By the time we tracked it to the new bank, he'd be gone, and he wouldn't take the chance of showing up in person."

"He'd have to authorize the outgoing wire transfer in writing, and that'd tell us in advance where the new account was. He'll go to the bank once, to withdraw the cash."

"We can't just let him waltz into the bank, fill out a withdrawal slip and take off."

"No, but we can make him think that's going to happen. Let me run a plan past you."

"Go ahead."

"What did he do as soon as he learned he couldn't get what he wanted by threatening you?"

"He blew up your car."

"Right. He threatened someone he figured you care about. He assumes you'd be scared for me, and we can use that against him."

"I am scared for you."

"Then you'll be all the more convincing."

"About what?"

"That you'll be sure he gets in the bank, withdraws his money, and gets away safe by using me as his hostage. He probably figures you'd risk your own life, but not someone else's, especially mine."

"I can't do that."

"Sure you can."

"If something happened to you, I couldn't live with myself."

Dave leaned across the desk and picked up her hand. "Nothing's going to happen. Now, let's work this out so you know what to say when he calls."

52

The park, adjacent to the Government Center, was full with its usual early morning assortment of county employees on break, rollerbladers, strollers, game-players, teenagers and transients.

The boy was about fourteen, white, clean cut, with a Jerry Rice jersey, baggy jeans, a 49ers cap turned backward, and a backpack. He sailed the Frisbee over a group of seniors setting up a game of lawn bowling. As the disk neared the pond, his black Lab timed its descent perfectly, leaped into the air, and caught it in her mouth. She trotted back, dropped the Frisbee at the boy's feet and looked up expectantly, drooling tongue hanging out the side of her mouth.

He sat on a bench near an Hispanic family spreading out a blanket for a picnic, crossed his ankles and drew deeply on his cigarette.

"Hey, kid."

The boy looked up. "Me?"

"Yeah. You wanna make twenty bucks?"

"How?"

"Let me play Frisbee with you an' yer dog."

The boy hesitated. "You're kidding, right?"

"Nope, just lonely. I haven't played Frisbee with my kid for a long time, he lives over in the Valley in Tulare with his mom."

He crooked his finger and motioned for the boy to come closer, and the ashes fell off his cigarette. He dropped the butt on the grass and ground it out with the toe of his cowboy boot, fished another from his plaid shirt pocket, flicked open his Zippo and lit up. As an afterthought, he extended the pack, but the boy declined.

"That's smart, these things'll kill ya." He coughed deep and spat a stringy glob of phlegm at the NO LITTERING *sign.*

"What's yer name, kid?"

"Tommy."

"Tommy what?"

"Rose."

"You any relation to that old-time baseball player?"

"I don't know."

He nodded his head toward Tommy's black Lab. "What's her name?"

"Sierra."

"She plays Frisbee real good. I'll give ya ten bucks now to play Frisbee with me an' Sierra, then another ten when I get tired of playin'." He handed a ten dollar bill to Tommy, who accepted it cautiously.

"Damn, alls I got left is a twenty. Guess I'll have to pay you thirty bucks total. How 'bout it?" He glanced at the window and noted that the light was on.

"Make up yer mind, kid."

"Okay."

He stuck the ear plug in his left ear and raised the mouthpiece to his lips.

"What's that?" Tommy asked.

"A telephone, I've gotta make a call while we play. Now, you and the dog run out there and I'll toss it to you."

He dropped his smoke on the lawn and flipped the Frisbee as hard as he could. It arched high over their heads, and landed in the brush along the river. He punched a local number into his cell phone.

"Hello."

"Have you unfroze my account?"

"Not yet, but I'm willing to talk about it."

"I hear an echo. Am I on a speaker phone, Mackay?"

"Yes."

The Frisbee came sailing back. He caught it and tossed it again, as far as he could.

"Is that asshole Granz with you?"

"Yes."

He caught the Frisbee and threw it again, speaking inconspicuously into the miniature mouthpiece. "No more talkin'. Unfreeze my bank account."

"I want the rest of the infants you and Fredericks abducted."

Sierra dropped the Frisbee at his feet. He patted her head and sailed it past a group of homeless men who were hassling two young women in shorts and halter tops.

He thought it over. "How do I know you won't take me out at the bank?"

"You take me with you as a hostage," Granz answered. "Once you get your money, you give me the location of the babies, drop me alongside the freeway someplace and disappear. I'm your insurance policy."

"If you fuck with me, I'll kill you."

"That's what I'd expect," Granz said.

"How do I know you won't come after me later?"

"You know where I am. You can carry out your threat anytime and I wouldn't know until it was too late."

"Damn right. Don't forget that, either."

"Do we have a deal or not?" Granz persisted.

He threw the Frisbee at the kid's head, but missed and Sierra chased it down.

"Tomorrow morning at seven o'clock, Granz. You start at the south county line and drive your car north on Highway One. Have Mackay's cell phone with you and turned on. If there aren't any other cops in cars, planes, choppers, or whatever, I'll contact you with instructions."

"I don't have a car, asshole. You blew it up."

"Rent a white Toyota Camry at Budget. See you tomorrow."

He disconnected the phone and lowered the mouthpiece. "Hey, Tommy."

"Yes, sir?" Tommy and the dog were panting and wheezing from chasing after the Frisbee.

"I'm tired, let's quit."

"Okay, gimme my money."

"What money?"

"You promised me another twenty dollars after we quit playing. I want it."

He pointed at the Government Center. "So, sue me, you little shit."

53

"It's almost noon, let's walk to the mall and get a sandwich."

"Okay."

Mackay and Granz exited the rear of the Government Center and walked toward downtown Santa Rita. "Were you able to rent a white Camry?" she asked.

"Enterprise had one."

"What did Escalante find out from the rest of the bank records?"

"Three fifty-thousand dollar deposits, in March and early April, probably finders' fees for our other three missing infants. She's trying to trace them."

"Down payments."

"You could call them that."

At Broccoli's Deli, Mackay ordered an egg salad sandwich and Granz an Italian meatball. They carried their food to a sidewalk table. Granz removed a sheet of paper from his inside coat pocket and slid it across the table.

"And that's not all," he explained before she could read it. "The May twenty-second, fifty-thousand dollar inter-branch transfer to Ledbetter came from Garrett and Gayle Alexander's account."

"What?!"

"According to Gayle Alexander, Janey was six weeks old when she was kidnapped. That means she was born around the middle of May, just before the Alexanders made the payment. They also paid Ledbetter fifty thousand on April fifteenth."

Mackay set her sandwich down. "Damn! They adopted her."

"You got it. They knew the DNA tests would reveal that they weren't the parents, that's why they weren't anxious to take polygraphs or have their blood tested."

"And why they refused to put up their own cash for the ransom, and why they never sounded anxious to get Janey back."

"The same reasons Gary Manoff isn't. The birthmark."

"Deborah Manoff's the only person who loves that baby for who she is, not what she looks like, and she'll probably never see Amanda—or Janey—again because of her asshole husband. Doesn't *any*body want that little girl?"

"Yeah, her birth parents."

"We have no idea who they are."

"Sure we do. As soon as the DNA results came

back, I ran an NCIC Missing Children check, looking for infant abductions anytime after May fifteenth."

"And?"

"A Caucasian female infant was abducted from a birthing center in San Antonio, Texas, on May nineteenth. She had a large port-wine stain on her torso. About three days later a female infant fitting that description was placed with the Alexanders for adoption. By Bernard Ledbetter."

"Jesus Christ, you know what that means?"

"Hell, yeah. She was abducted first from her natural parents in Texas and sold to the Alexanders for a hundred thousand dollars, kidnapped again, ransomed for two million bucks, and resold to the Manoffs."

"This is unbelievable."

"Believe it. That's what happened."

"What do you know about the real parents?"

"He's a professor at the university and she's a graphic artist. That's all I've found out so far."

"Let's talk to the Alexanders."

"You want me to call and set up a time for them to come to your office?"

"And let them cook up another batch of BS? Let's drive out there right now and drop in unannounced."

"Have we committed a crime, Lieutenant Granz? If so, I'd like to call our attorney."

Garrett Alexander seemed unaffected by the news, but Gayle Alexander cleared her throat repeatedly. They sat at opposite ends of the sofa.

Granz started the recorder. "Neither of you is suspected of any criminal behavior, Mr. Alexander. Private adoptions aren't illegal in California, nor is paying reasonable placement fees and the natural mother's medical costs. We just want to positively identify Janey. Why didn't you tell us Janey was adopted when you first reported her missing?"

The Alexanders looked at each other. "Mr. Ledbetter told us not to, that the fees we paid were technically illegal, and we could get in a lot of trouble if anyone found out."

"Did Ledbetter ever tell you how he located infants for adoption?" Mackay asked.

Gayle answered. "He said he worked with Right-to-Life organizations, Janey's mother was a high school student who refused to identify the baby's father, and that he made a secrecy agreement with the girl's parents to not divulge the baby's origin."

"When did she arrive?" Granz asked.

"May twenty-third," Gayle Alexander replied.

"The first fifty-thousand dollar payment you made to Bernard Ledbetter in April was a search fee?"

"Yes," Garrett answered.

"And the one on the twenty-second was the placement fee?"

"That's right, we paid it a day or so before Mr. Spade delivered her to the house."

Mackay and Granz looked at each other. "You spoke with Mr. Spade?"

"Just once, the night he and his assistant brought Janey."

Mackay handed the Alexanders a photograph of Monica Fredericks. "Is this one of the people who brought Janey?"

"That's one of them. I couldn't see him very well, but he was a big man. He talked in a gravelly voice and smelled like cigarettes."

"Did you see the car?" Granz asked.

"Yes, it was a big black thing like a Land Rover."

"A Chevy Suburban?"

"It could have been."

"Could you identify the man if you saw him again?"

She shook her head. "Maybe—it was dark."

Granz turned to Garrett Alexander. "How about you, could you identify the man?"

"I hadn't got home from work yet when she arrived. Now, have we answered all your questions?"

"For the moment," Granz told them, "but we may want to talk to you again."

"No problem."

The Alexanders started to stand, but Gayle sat back down. "What happens to Janey now, Ms. Mackay?"

"I don't know."

54

"Hi, babe, it's me. Did I wake you?"

"I tossed and turned all night. I gave it up at about four-thirty."

"How come you couldn't sleep?"

"Christ, Dave, you know why! He's a goddamn murderer."

"I know, but why lose sleep over it?"

"I suppose you slept?"

"Yep. I think I'll stop at Starbucks for coffee and a scone. Why don't you join me, my treat? It may be the last time you get me to buy."

"Dammit, don't joke around."

"What do you expect me to do, admit I'm scared, apologize for the shit I stirred up between you and me, tell you I love you? Well, I am, I do, and I do. Now, how about coffee?"

"I can't leave Emma by herself."

"Okay."

"Dave?"

"Yeah."

"Be careful."

"I will."

The apartment was in a high-density, multiple dwelling-unit subdivision, making it easy to park unnoticed among the cars that spilled over from the shoulder-to-shoulder apartment and condo complex parking lots into the streets.

At 6:30 A.M., Granz walked casually to the Camry, stopped, stretched and yawned, leaned against the car and talked briefly on a cell phone, then climbed in the car and pulled out of the carport.

He noted Granz' clothing; tan Dockers, pale blue polo shirt, cordovan Rockport loafers; tossed a cigarette butt out the window on a pile of others, and followed at a discreet distance.

Several blocks later, he zipped down a residential side street parallel to Granz' route and accelerated to sixty to beat Granz, passing rows of houses where people were showering and eating breakfasts before heading for work.

"Fuckin' lemmings." He lit another smoke and pulled the stolen RX-7 into the Starbucks lot, parked next to Granz's rented Toyota, and strode inside wearing a chocolate brown UPS driver's uniform with S. SPADE *on a nameplate.*

Spade drizzled cream and sugar into his coffee while he watched Granz wait for his espresso, then headed for South County.

At 6:45, Granz drove into Monterey County on Highway 1 and turned around at the first access road intersection. Backtracking, he slowed as he approached the Santa Rita County line, pulled onto the shoulder, and parked beside the county limit sign. He left the engine running, checked Mackay's cell phone and set it on the passenger seat, then popped a chunk of maple scone into his mouth and flipped the top off his coffee cup.

At 7:00 A.M., he slipped the car into drive and merged into light northbound traffic, driving slowly in the right lane, anticipating last-minute instructions. They came within the first mile.

He picked up the phone. "Granz."

"Pull into the center median and stop immediately!"

Granz complied. "Now what?"

"Put your coffee down and grab Mackay's cell phone. Do you see the temporary construction sign?"

"Yeah."

"Turn the phone off and carry it to the sign."

As he approached the huge orange sign, Granz heard a cell phone chirp, looked around, then stooped and picked up a plastic bag that contained a cellular phone and a roll of electrical tape. He removed the phone and answered it. "Go."

"Tape Mackay's phone to the signpost as near the top as possible, with the antenna pointing up."

Granz worked for a minute, then reported, "Done."

"Turn Mackay's phone on and dial seven-six-seven-eight-nine-hundred, then take the other phone and go back to the car."

James Fields and Donna Escalante sat on stools in the Santa Rita County Multi-Agency Emergency Communications Center.

"How accurately can you pinpoint Lieutenant Granz's position from the cell phone?" Escalante asked a technician. "The hand-held Global Positioning System unit I carry when I hike in wilderness areas is accurate within a couple of feet."

"This isn't like GPS, it's low-tech. We triangulate on phone transmissions from three antennas; one on the Government Center, one on Mt. Cabrillo, and the third in South County."

"So, how close can you get?"

"We tested it this morning outside Granz' apartment, and again as he drove south on Highway One. He described where he was while we tracked the movement and verified our triangulation. We were about a hundred yards off."

"A lot could go wrong in a hundred yards."

"I know, and we can only triangulate when the phone's on, and if Granz doesn't talk long enough, we—woops, what's going on?"

Fields and Escalante crowded around the technician. "What?" Fields asked.

"The phone's been transmitting continuously from a fixed location near the county line for almost five minutes."

"Meaning?" Escalante asked.

"Either Granz is carrying on a long conversation or something's wrong. His earlier conversations were short and sweet, or from a moving car."

"Shit! Could the phone have been dumped?"

"Not likely, we're still tracking him."

"Not any more."

* * *

"All right, Granz, so far so good. Do what I tell you, and I won't squeeze the trigger and blow a big ugly hole in that pretty blue shirt."

"Fuck you," Granz replied.

"Very funny. Now, let exactly twenty northbound vehicles pass, then continue north on Highway One until I contact you again."

"Let's get on with it," Granz said.

"Be patient, the bank's not open yet. And be a good boy or the next thing Mackay'll hear will be the bomb that blows you and a dozen others to hell."

The twentieth vehicle was a ten-wheeler loaded with lettuce, headed for a cooling plant. Granz settled in behind it, and the phone chirped almost immediately.

"Take the first exit and follow the truck. Stop at the second set of railroad tracks at the apple processing plant."

A minute later, Granz reported. "I'm there."

"Wait five minutes, then retrace your route, except go under the freeway and answer the pay phone at the Chevron station. Don't fuck up."

"You take care of your business, I'll take care of mine, asshole."

He dialed the pay phone when Granz pulled into the service station and stopped beside the RX-7.

"Yeah," Granz answered.

"Describe what you see across the road."

"A field of bush berries. The rows run perpendicular to the highway and about half the length of the field to the

south, there are two wooden stakes with red flags on them. Beyond the field is the water treatment plant."

"The flags mark a road used by berry pickers' trucks. Drive up that road and stop when you can't go any farther. Stay in the car and leave the phone on."

Granz swung the Toyota into the narrow, deeply rutted dirt road and idled up between the rows of trellised berry vines, which scraped along the sides of the car as they encroached into the lane. About two hundred feet in, he slammed on the brakes and skidded to a dusty stop behind a blue Jeep Cherokee.

"Granz, can you hear me?" the phone asked.

"I hear you."

"Clasp your hands on top of your head and climb out of the car. Face the Jeep, drop to your knees and cross your ankles."

"It's showtime, Granz. Turn around or do anything dumb, you're a dead man. I sorta wish you'd try something, but don't, 'cause I need my money."

He dropped a bag on the ground and removed a black stocking cap, which he slid over Granz' head so it covered his eyes, nose and mouth. "Can you see?"

Granz' voice was muffled. "No."

"Good. Now hold real still while I check you for weapons."

The stun gun was about the size of a pack of cigarettes, and less than a third as thick. He had taped it to his upper thigh, under his scrotum, knowing that most men wouldn't check there. It was one of the first things they taught at the police academy—always check the suspect's crotch. He held his breath. Marlboro Man checked under his arms for a shoulder holster, but nowhere else.

He's been watching too much television, Granz thought. "I'm not packing," he said. "Even you're not stupid enough to forget to search me."

"Tell me whether you recognize this sound," Marlboro Man said, then jacked a shell into the chamber of the new twelve-gauge Remington pump shotgun and released the safety.

"Damn right I recognize it."

He pulled the end of a fresh roll of duct tape and started working, wrapping tape around Granz' waist, chest and neck.

"What're you doing?" Granz demanded.

"Taping the shotgun up the middle of your back, so the muzzle's pointed at the base of your skull. Then I'm gonna handcuff you and you're gonna lie on the backseat of the Jeep while we take a ride to the bank."

"I can't breathe through this cap all the way to Santa Clara."

"I'll take it off as soon as we're on our way, but if. . . ."

"I already know what'll happen if I screw up, asshole."

Kathryn grabbed her phone on the first ring. "Mackay."

"This is Escalante."

"What's wrong?"

"County Comm lost the trace on your cell phone. A patrol deputy found it taped to a signpost, connected to a PacBell time recording. The Camry was abandoned in a berry field a mile from the phone and torched with a delayed-fuse pipe bomb taped to a gasoline can."

"Was . . ."

"Lieutenant Granz wasn't in the car."

Mackay sighed deeply. "What about the stun gun and tracking device?"

"They weren't in the Camry or with the phone. We're assuming he still has them."

"Let's hope so."

55

Fields piloted his Mercury Cougar as fast as the sharp turns and steep grade of the old highway permitted. When it crested a hill, Escalante plugged her cellular phone into the lighter and dialed.

"Mackay."

"This is Escalante. Fields and I are en route to Santa Clara."

"Brief me."

"CHP Officer Starling staged a wreck at the summit to slow traffic. We'll get to the bank before they do."

"Video cameras in place?"

"Yeah, three. CHP is squeezing northbound traffic through the accident scene into one lane, so cars will pass close by the CHP unit and tow truck. One camera's on each side and one's mounted on the tow truck boom, looking down into the interior of the cars as they go by. The cameras have zoom lenses and remotes, so if a car passes with Granz inside, they'll record it and give detectives on the monitors a good look at both of them, and the car."

"Is everything ready at the bank?"

"Sergeant Miller moved S.O.'s mobile command post over last night and set up in an RV dealer's lot across the street. Santa Clara P.D. sealed off the area, and planted a few undercover cars in the parking lot. Bank personnel were given the day off with pay. Manager was a pain in the ass, said she wanted to stay in case we needed someone who knows about banking, but I nixed that. Female S.R.S.O. deputies'll be at the teller cages and I'll be behind the manager's desk. Two plainclothes detectives will be inside posing as customers."

"How about the SWAT team?"

"They were deployed to the bank before dawn. They left one sniper at the accident scene in case the perp spooks and tries to flee."

"Inspector, it's your job to make sure nobody spooks him."

"Yes, ma'am, I will."

"You will."

He tapped his left foot in time with the music and turned down the volume. "I better, 'cause if I don't walk away from that bank alive, neither do you."

"I'm a dead man, anyway, especially if you keep smoking those damn cigarettes with all the windows rolled up."

He laughed, coughed, rolled down the driver's window, spat, lit another cigarette and closed the window. "I ain't decided yet."

"Bull shit."

"Then I oughta blow you away right now and get it over with, wise guy." He slammed on the brakes and swerved toward the right shoulder.

"You'll never see a penny of your money."

He laughed again and swerved the Jeep back onto the roadway. "You ain't as dumb as you look, Granz. What the fuck—"

Granz lay in the rear seat, knees bent, handcuffed in front, with the cuff chain looped under his belt, which was rotated with the buckle in back, under the shotgun. He had obtained some relief from the weapon pressing into his spine by lying partially on his side, but feared that too much movement would trigger the loaded, cocked shotgun.

The stocking cap was rolled up above his nose so he could breathe, but still covered his eyes. Granz had carefully counted minutes and interpreted the motion of the vehicle when it left South County, passed the FishHook, and climbed over the freeway toward San Jose. By his calculations, they should be approaching the spot where traffic would start to slow due to Marlon Starling's accident.

"What the fuck—"

He braked sharply to avoid crashing into the car in front of the Jeep, then crept forward with the traffic. A road sign with flashing yellow letters said, CAUTION - - - ACCIDENT AHEAD.

"Just what th' fuck I need," he grumbled. Gradually, he nudged the Jeep forward, car length at a time, until he spotted the fire truck, tow truck, ambulance and CHP

cars a quarter mile ahead. He switched the radio from the crackling, fading Salinas oldies station to a country music station and turned up the volume.

"Well, there ain't nothin' I can do, so might as well enjoy some good music. "Willie Nelson's my favorite."

Willie was singing "You Were Always On My Mind."

Surreptitiously, Granz unzipped his fly and squirmed around until he could slide his right hand inside his pants. He pushed a finger under the elastic leg on his briefs, and felt around, wishing for the first time that he wore boxers.

"Hey! What th' fuck you doin', jackin' off back there?"

"I've got an itch, and I need to take a leak," Granz told him. "What do you care?"

Spade laughed. "I don't, I just figured you had more class than most cops, that you'd rather play with yerself in private. And don't piss on the seat, either. If you don't gimme any shit, I'll let you drain the lizard when we get to the bank."

Granz located an adhesive bandage nestled in his pubic hair, slid his index finger under it and flipped the switch. "I can wait."

"The homing device just activated." A detective in the surveillance unit disguised as an ambulance pushed the head phones tight against his ears to confirm the signal, and grabbed a hand-held radio. "Hey, Gordo."

A heavy-set detective dressed as a tow truck driver answered. "Go."

"I just picked up Granz' beeper. Start the camera."

"Check."

"Roll the cameras," he ordered two other detectives, one in a van parked on the shoulder, the other in one of the wrecked cars, a narc undercover Corvette.

" 'Bout fuckin' time," he grumbled as the Jeep approached the accident. "Jesus Christ, would you look at that, one of the wrecks is a brand new Corvette roadster. I'll bet the asshole that owns it's pissed. Fuckin' commuters don't know how to drive fer shit. Glad I don't have to commute to work every fuckin' day."

He laughed and coughed. "I set my own hours, that's what I like best about my occupation."

Granz didn't comment, but heard police radios, idling engines, and a tow truck's cable running out.

"Don't move or say shit, Granz, we're about to pass the CHP car. Screw up, a lotta people are gonna die right here, and yer gonna be first."

"I'm not going anywhere," Granz assured him, then made a minute movement with his hand and extended thumb. A moment later, he felt the Jeep accelerate.

"We're home free," he said. "Next stop, CalWestern Bank."

"Mackay."

"This is Escalante. CHP advises that Lieutenant Granz is in the back seat of a white '98 Jeep Cherokee, stolen in Saratoga last night. It just passed through the Summit checkpoint."

"Is . . . ?"

"He's handcuffed and a stocking cap's pulled

over his eyes, but he gave a little thumbs-up for the cameras as they passed the accident. He's okay."

"How long to the bank?"

"Twenty minutes, max. Two unmarked Santa Clara S.O. units are now a half-mile ahead of them on the freeway, and will stay with them all the way to the bank. Two of our S.O. units are following at a distance."

"One way or another, it's almost over," Mackay observed softly.

"Almost," Escalante agreed.

Granz located two plastic bandages, one on the inside of each thigh, just beneath his scrotum. He pulled one and stripped the adhesive away from his leg, ripping off skin and hair at the same time. Pressing it against his leg and working clumsily with one hand, he opened the tiny scissors of the Swiss Army pocketknife. Sweat accumulated under the cap and ran down his cheeks, but he didn't notice.

"You still fiddlin' with yerself back there?"

"Fuck you."

Working the tiny, spring-loaded scissors with his right thumb and forefinger, he laboriously cut through the remaining adhesive tape that wrapped completely around his upper thigh, two layers thick. He peeled back the tape and pulled the stun gun loose, activated it, tucked it into the waistband of his trousers, then zipped his fly closed.

"You finished, Granz?"

"Almost."

56

Flanked by a dry cleaner and a used-book store whose owners had agreed to stay open late, the Santa Clara CalWestern Bank occupied the center of an old three-unit cinder block strip mall a half block south of Interstate 880. To the chagrin of modern city planners, it survived as an unsightly monument to the 1950 and 60's growth that swept through the Santa Clara Valley like wildfire, leaving irreversible blight in its wake.

James Fields fed the wire from his back pocket under his shirt, up the left side of his neck, stuck the ear-plug in his left ear and clipped the mini-microphone under his shirt collar. He glanced across the street at the 39 foot Pace Arrow Vision, whose drawn windshield covers obscured the vehicle's interior.

"Jazzbo, you hear me okay?"

"Loud and clear." Miller manned the surveillance and communication console inside the motor home that S.R.S.O. had confiscated under the asset forfeiture laws during a drug bust.

Satisfied he could communicate with the command post, Fields sat down outside the bank's entrance and leaned against the wall, feet in the gutter. He wore one dirty white Reebok and one scuffed cordovan wingtip, dingy jeans, and a ragged long-sleeve plaid shirt with the right sleeve folded up and pinned, to accent his missing hand and lower arm.

A partially full wine bottle and a Rubbermaid container with several one-dollar bills in it sat beside him on the sidewalk with a sign:

Vietnam Vet Homeless
Hungry and Hopeless
Please Help
(bills, only, no coins)

"How 'bout you, Escalante?"

In defiance of management's best efforts, the bank's interior was a drab square box with three teller stations, a few desks and a safe whose door was visible behind the center teller. Escalante stood at the counter where customers filled out deposit and withdrawal slips, behind a partition to the right of the glass door.

"Loud and clear," Escalante answered.

"You hear her, Miller?"

"Yep."

"Are you in position, Escalante?"

"He won't spot me until after they enter. Once they're inside, I'll control the exit."

"Okay, Miller, Escalante, we're the only ones on

channel-A. Jazzbo, keep up a running commentary on what's happening, starting when you see the Jeep turn off the freeway, until they enter the bank. As of now, we won't respond unless something goes wrong."

"Ten-four."

Fields sat back to wait for the action to start. He didn't wait long.

"They just left the freeway," Miller said calmly into the radio, ". . . heading up the street at about fifteen MPH. I see the driver but not Granz. They're slowing down, stand by . . ."

A few yards from the mall's driveway, the Jeep slowed and stopped, waited two or three minutes, then pulled into the parking lot, swung around and backed into a stall in front of the bookstore.

Miller's monotone whispered through Fields's and Escalante's earphones.

"They just parked," Miller intoned. "Driver's sitting still, he . . . he just rolled down the driver's window, now he's leaning his head out, I think he's listening. No sign of Granz. Wait . . . wait."

Fields felt his body tense and forced himself to relax and lean over, as if he were already drunk.

"Driver turning around—he's saying something toward the back seat. Now he's leaning over, doing something with . . . looks like a piece of rope—in the rear seat."

The radio was silent for a few seconds.

"Okay, here we go, the left rear door is opening but no one . . . hold on, hold on, someone's moving around in the back seat."

Fields and Escalante heard Miller speak into the tactical channel. "S-1, report."

SWAT sniper-1 was posted on the RV dealer's roof. "Roger, the Jeep's left rear door open," he responded softly, "but no line of sight to the driver."

"S-2?" Miller inquired.

SWAT sniper-2 peered cautiously over the ledge of the dry cleaner's roof, to the Jeep's right. "Rear seat movement, unknown nature of the activity."

Suddenly, Granz' feet extended past the Jeep's left rear door and dropped to the pavement. He pulled himself upright, stood, staggered, and leaned against the side of the vehicle. The stocking cap was pulled down past his chin, a length of yellow polypropylene rope was looped around his neck, and he was cuffed with his hands behind his back.

The rope yanked tight, and Granz pushed himself away from the car then backed slowly toward the driver's door, which swung open. A hand emerged holding a nine millimeter automatic pistol pointed at the back of Granz' head. The rest of Marlboro Man followed and stood beside his hostage, cautiously surveying the scene.

"Fuck!" Miller watched until he was sure, then said into the TAC channel, "S-units, DO NOT FIRE, repeat, DO NOT FIRE! Acknowledge."

"S-One, check."

"S-two, check."

Miller spoke into the channel-A microphone. "Subject is in jeans and a dark blue shirt. He's wearing body armor outside the shirt. Granz' eyes are covered. He has a rope around his neck and the other end's tied around the subject's left wrist. Looks like some kind of weapon's taped to his back. S-one, can you confirm?"

Several seconds elapsed while the SWAT sniper adjusted his rifle's telescopic sight.

"S-one, affirmative. Looks like a twelve gauge shotgun. The barrel's taped to Granz' neck, muzzle against his head. Subject's finger's inside the trigger guard and the safety's released. If that fucking shotgun's loaded. If he squeezes that trigger, he'll blow Granz' head off."

"Fields," Miller said softly into Channel-A, "key your mike twice if you copied S-1."

Fields depressed his mike button two times.

"Okay," Miller said, "Change of plans. If SWAT takes the subject out, he might squeeze off the shotgun before he drops."

Miller paused to consider the situation, then continued, "You'll have to play it by ear once they get inside. Copy?"

Fields punched his mike button twice in rapid succession, as did Escalante.

"Here they come," Miller reported. "Suspect and hostage are moving toward the bank. Suspect's behind the hostage, rope in left hand, the right's on the shotgun. They're crossing the parking lot. Fifty feet . . . forty . . . thirty . . . twenty. They're rounding the corner of the building . . . command post out."

"Hey, Gimp!"

Fields looked up. His left hand trembled, but he

managed to raise the Thunderbird bottle to his lips and swallow, then spilled some on his shirt.

"Huh?"

"I'm talkin' to you, gimp. You a fuckin' cop?"

"Huh?"

Marlboro Man studied Fields closely. "You better not be or you're a dead gimp. I'm a 'Nam vet myself, so just sit there and drink and you won't get hurt."

"Huh?"

Fields waited until he heard the bank door hiss closed, then counted to twenty, and slipped off his mismatched shoes. He set the wine bottle down and stood, withdrew his automatic weapon, dragged in a deep breath and opened the bank door.

57

He stuck the pistol under his body armor and stepped inside the bank. The door swung closed behind him, and he moved to the side, back against the wall adjacent to the door. One hand tugged at the rope, keeping Granz' body in front of his as a shield, while the other gripped the shotgun.

No one noticed.

To his right, a woman teller was cashing an elderly man's Social Security check, while another counted currency from a canvas merchant deposit bag. Across the aisle, a pregnant black woman leaned over the manager's desk discussing art work selections for her new checks. Detective Rachel Ward was working her last week before going out on maternity leave.

"Listen up!" He waited until everyone looked his direction. "Stay calm. Don't move unless I tell you, and no one'll get hurt."

He turned toward the teller cages. "Don't push any alarm buttons, and put your hands on the counter where I can see them. And you, pregnant bitch! Put your hands on top of your head. Move around the desk and sit on the floor with your back against the wall."

He instructed both tellers to do the same, then ordered the elderly customer, Sheriff's Deputy Rod O'Connor, "You, too, geezer! Go!" Then he added, "And take your money with you, you old fart, you prob'ly need it worse than I do."

Granz surreptitiously raised his shirttail, unclipped the mini stun gun from his waistband and switched it on. The capacitors whined softly as they charged the unit from two tiny batteries, but the Marlboro Man didn't hear.

Through horn-rimmed glasses that magnified her dark eyes to the size of saucers, Escalante watched Granz arm himself, then nod his head slightly. Smaller than a pack of cigarettes, the 80,000-volt Talon packed a powerful punch, but Escalante figured Granz would only get one chance, and she had seen grown men take 200,000 volts without going down.

He shoved Granz in front of him to the manager's desk and stopped. "I wanna make a withdrawal."

In her peripheral vision, Escalante watched Fields silently open and close the bank's front door, draw his service weapon, and drop to one knee.

"Go to hell," she said.

As fast and hard as his shackled wrists permitted, Granz thrust the stun gun backward. He felt the man spasm, squeezed his eyes shut, and waited for the shotgun to go off. Nothing happened. The stun gun whined and recharged, and Granz jammed it into his captor's crotch a second time. Then, he ducked.

One probe smashed into his left testicle, buckling his knees; the second caught the glans penis. He screamed as eighty-thousand volts of artificial, man-made lightning shot through his manhood. He knew a low-voltage stun gun's effects lasted just a few seconds and fought to remain conscious, but the jolt had disrupted the electrical signals from his brain and it forgot how to control his muscles.

Dazed and disoriented, his hands and arms refused to follow instructions to retrieve the 9mm pistol from under his bulletproof vest. He started counting backward from one hundred to clear his mind. When he reached ninety, he urinated in his pants and fell to the floor.

He felt the pistol under his vest pressing against his chest as the shotgun exploded.

Granz heard the blast, then a deafening ringing in his ears. His face and neck felt like they were on fire, but when he ran his hands over them and felt no blood or raw flesh he knew he wasn't badly hurt.

Escalante grabbed a pair of scissors from the desk, ran to Granz, yanked off the stocking cap, quickly hacked away the duct tape, and slipped him her second service weapon, a .25 caliber Beretta, which she pulled from an ankle holster.

The shotgun clattered to the floor out of reach. His arms finally obeyed and he slid the pistol from under his vest, opened one eye cautiously, and spotted the bank manager stooped over Granz. He lunged and grabbed Escalante's ankle, yanking her feet out from under her. She collapsed to the floor and he pounced on her, jammed the muzzle of the nine-millimeter in her ear and when he glanced around he saw Granz roll over and reach for the shotgun.

"Don't even think about it," he screamed, then stood on shaky legs and dragged Escalante up with him, squeezing his body close to hers for protection.

"Granz, you double-crossing cocksucker, this shoulda gone smooth as a baby's ass. Nobody 'cept you had to die." He spun and fired toward the wall where the pregnant woman, the old codger and the teller were crouched, pointing guns at him. The bullet splashed into Rachel Ward's distended stomach with a sickening liquid thud.

He turned back to Granz. "Now, you sonofabitch, I'm gonna blow you and this Mexican cunt away."

"I don't think so," Fields said.

"What, the—" he whirled, stared, then grinned. "I shoulda known, you one-arm gimp." He pressed the pistol tight against Escalante's head.

"Say adios, Chiquita."

Fields squeezed off two quick rounds. The first hollow point slug entered Marlboro Man's right side and started to spin him around, but the second stopped him, shattering his left shoulder in the process. He groaned and sat straight down, but remained upright. His jaws moved and his eyes said, "I can still fight," but his body refused. The pistol fell into his lap and slid to the floor.

Granz ran over and kicked the pistol away, then knelt and yanked open the man's shirt to assess the damage. Bone protruded from the shattered shoulder but wasn't life threatening. He checked the other wound and turned to Fields. "Get me some towels from the bathroom for a compression bandage. Quick!"

When Fields returned, Granz folded the towels quickly and shoved the bandage under the man's shirt over the torso wound and leaned heavily on it with his left palm. He made eye contact with Fields and shook his head "no" almost imperceptibly.

Fields understood. "I'll get the paramedics."

"No!" Granz shouted, and released the pressure on the bandage.

"Whadaya mean, 'no'?"

"I think I'll let him die."

Fields shrugged and knelt beside Granz. "Good idea."

Marlboro Man's eyes darted frantically from Granz to Fields, then back. "Jesus—"

"Shut up and listen." Granz resumed pressure on the pressure bandage. "Here's how it's gonna work. I'll ask you a few simple questions. Give me the right answers, I keep pressure on the bandages. You don't and I pull these towels out and walk away. You'll bleed to death before the paramedics get here. Understand?"

Marlboro Man nodded.

"Where are the other babies? Names, addresses, everything."

"My wallet."

Fields grabbed the damaged shoulder, eliciting a scream, rolled him onto his back, pulled out the wallet, and dropped him back to the floor with a thud. He pulled out a grubby piece of paper which, unfolded, was half a sheet off a yellow legal pad. He read it and passed it to Granz, who studied it and handed it back.

"Too easy," Granz said. "Why keep a written record in your wallet?"

Marlboro Man groaned. "Only safe place. Figured I'd need it someday."

"For blackmailing the kids' new parents?"

"Not the parents, the *Man*."

"Don't jerk me around or I'll pull this towel out right now. You worked for someone else?"

Marlboro Man grabbed Granz' hand and pushed it against the bandage. When he pulled it back it was covered with blood. "Right. This is big."

"Bullshit," Granz spat, his skepticism belying a gut instinct that he was hearing the truth. "Who'd you take orders from?"

"Cunt lawyer in New York. Mean bitch."

Granz frowned. "You said 'The *Man*.' "

"Big boss lives out of the country. Moves around."

"How do you know that?"

Marlboro Man's eyes rolled and he groaned. "Fuck, Granz, I hurt bad. Get me some pain meds."

Granz shook his head. "Keep talking."

"Staked out Ledbetter. Seen this guy come and go, so I leaned on Ledbetter. He said the guy's an old client, worked at a public clinic in Frisco a few years back. Ledbetter did adoptions, the doc supplied babies from his clinic. Later, they hired me to snatch kids from them midwife places. The doc knew all about 'em."

"So you kept a list to hit them up for more cash."

"Fuckin'-A."

"Tell me the doc's name."

"Not till I see paramedics."

Granz nodded at Fields, who stood and walked outside. Within a minute he was back, followed by two paramedics pushing a gurney. Granz kept pressure on the bandage while they loaded the injured man and started to wheel him toward the door.

"What's the doc's name?" Granz asked again.

Marlboro Man glared. "Simmons."

"You're fucking with me!" Granz yanked out the bloody bandage and tossed it to the floor.

"Jesus Christ! God damn you, Granz! Do something before I bleed to death!" he screamed at the paramedics.

Fields snorted.

One of the paramedics, a young woman, peeled open the man's shirt and looked inside. "You're not going to die," she told him. "It's only a flesh wound. The bleeding's already stopped."

"District Attorney Mackay's office."

"Jeanette, this is Inspector Escalante. Is Ms. Mackay available?"

"She's in court, Inspector. Shall I page her?"

"No, tell her I'm finished and on my way back in."

58

"All she said was she's on her way back?" Mackay asked.

"Yes, ma'am."

"Thanks, Jeanette. Hold my calls, please, and no interruptions till further notice."

Mackay closed her office door and dialed two more numbers. She let them ring several times, but neither Fields nor Escalante answered.

She tried to read the Juvenile Justice Commission's report on juvenile hall overcrowding, but couldn't concentrate. At ten minutes before twelve, she was startled by her office door opening.

"Jeanette, I asked you to—"

"Hi, babe, you busy?"

Except for a gauze pad over his ear and neck, Dave Granz looked no different than when he left home that morning.

Kathryn felt like crying, but forced herself not to.

"Dammit, Granz, you should have called to let me know everything went all right."

She didn't resist when he closed the door behind himself, walked to her chair, bent over and kissed her cheek. He sat in one of her leather chairs and leaned forward. "Everything *didn't* go all right, Kate," he said, then he told her about Rachel Ward.

"Is she—?"

"At the hospital in Santa Clara. The ER doc said she'll be okay, but she might lose the baby."

"Damn!"

"There *is* some good news," he continued, then showed her the slip of paper from Marlboro Man's wallet, then explained about Simmons.

She stared at the ceiling, which was littered with HVAC ducts, conduit and water pipes and sprayed with an acoustical cover, remaining motionless so long that Granz asked, "Kate?"

She pointed at his bandage. "How bad is that?"

"It's nothing. Gunpowder stipling. My biggest complaint is the ringing in my ears caused by the shotgun blast. Tinnitus—it'll go away. Let's talk about Simmons, Kate."

"What's to talk about? I'm going to catch the sonofabitch."

Granz started to say that catching criminals was his job and prosecuting them was hers, but let it go. Instead, he said, "We'll talk later, I've got work to do."

Just before 3 o'clock that afternoon, Escalante sat across her boss's desk and crossed one leg over the other. "Marlboro Man's name is Michael John Galbraith," she said. "Fifty-seven years old, ex-Army Ranger, weapons and explosives expert. Purple Heart from Vietnam, came back addicted, did some time at Folsom—forgery, embezzlement, grand theft. Big guy, six-six, two-thirty. Army records say his IQ is near-genius."

Mackay pushed aside the legal pad on which she was taking notes. "Okay. Get saliva samples from him and send them to DOJ for comparison to the swabs from the dead infant's mouth and the cigarette butts recovered from the crime scenes. If he gives you any shit, let me know and I'll get Judge Tucker to issue an order."

"Will do," Escalante assured her.

"What about the babies?"

Normally stoic, Escalante smiled broadly. "They're in protective custody as we speak."

"All of them? How did you—"

"The names and addresses from Galbraith's wallet matched the other fifty-thousand dollar deposits into Ledbetter's bank account. Lieutenant Granz contacted police in Phoenix, Cheyenne and Boise. I contacted Child Protective Services in each city and explained the situation. Actually, I leaned on them pretty heavy—told them if they waited for a court order, the babies would disappear and they'd be held responsible. They cooperated. You might need to clean up the legal and political messes I created, but I figured you'd agree it was worth it."

"Absolutely." Mackay thought for a moment, then

picked up the phone. "Would you please excuse me, Inspector, I need to arrange a media announcement."

Kathryn paged Dave fifteen minutes later. "I'll be on a special edition of *Larry King* at seven o'clock. His producer arranged a remote from Channel Six in Salinas."

"Great." He paused. "Are you taking Emma with you?"

She slapped her forehead. "No, she'll go to Ruth's."

"How about I pick Em up. She and I can go to the beach for an hour or so, then grab a bite to eat and be home in time to watch *Larry King*."

"I suppose that'd be okay."

59

"Neat car." Emma dug her bare toes into the carpet.

"Thanks."

"When I start driving I want a red BMW."

Dave zipped into the South County Pacific Pescadores Community Bank lot, pulled the rented Buick into the drive-up ATM, entered his code and stuck some cash into his shirt pocket.

"How much money did you get?"

"A hundred bucks."

"That's enough. I want to eat at the Cement Boat snack shack and go to Baskin-Robbins later."

He idled the car down the steep slope and paid four dollars to enter the state park, plus another two dollars to park. "Jeez, Emma, doesn't your mom ever feed you?"

"Sometimes. How come you got it, anyhow?"

"Because you're almost a teenager and eat more than a racehorse. I didn't think you'd settle for hay."

"I meant the Buick. What happened to your Explorer?"

"Your mom didn't tell you?"

"She never tells me nothing."

"*Anything*," he corrected.

"What?"

"*Anything*—she never tells me *anything*."

"Me either. Can I use your cell phone?"

"What for?"

"To call Ashley and find out what she's going to wear the first day back to school."

"That's not until August."

"I know, but it's important, Dave, please!"

"Sorry, I didn't bring it with me," he lied. He surveyed the crowded parking lot that separated the beach from the sheer vertical cliffs, from which the park's name derived, and parked in a red zone beside the visitor center. He shut off the engine and slid a "police vehicle" placard under the windshield wiper.

The afternoon sun was already becoming obscured by fog, but the beach was still crowded with blankets, umbrellas and sun worshipers. A narrow grass strip nestled at the base of the cliffs adjoined two dozen picnic tables and barbecue pits, whose sizzling hamburgers and chicken permeated the air with a tantalizing aroma.

"What should we do first?" he joked.

"Eat!"

Dave pulled a brochure from a dispenser on the side of the visitor center. "Let's learn about the boat, then grab some food and carry it out onto the wharf."

"Mom makes me sit at the table to eat. She says it's uncivilized otherwise."

"We won't tell her. Besides, we need to be home by seven to catch her on TV."

They ordered hamburgers, curly garlic fries and Cokes, and walked onto the wooden wharf that led to the boat's stern, past a colorful kiosk which sat in front of a sign that said, FRIENDS OF THE PALO ALTO DONATION STATION AND INFORMATION.

Dave swallowed a mouthful of burger, stuffed several fries in behind it and told Emma, "The brochure says that a few years ago, they started raising money to rebuild the *Palo Alto*. The first phase of the work's done, so they're celebrating this weekend."

"Why did they back the ship in when they parked it?" Emma asked.

He glanced at the brochure and frowned. "Good question, but it doesn't say in here and I don't know, either."

While they leaned against the railing eating, a two-man, two-woman Dixieland band, wearing bright red pants and peppermint-striped shirts, played. Nearby, four members of a barbershop quartet with frilly sleeve garters and straw hats waited their turn to entertain the crowd, many of whom were dancing in front of the umbrella-covered bandstand.

When they finished eating, Dave suggested they walk out onto the ship itself. "Em," he started hesitantly, "I'd like to ask you something."

"About you and Mom?"

"Well . . . yes, and about you and me, too."

"Okay."

Dave cleared his throat. "Remember when you and I went to the Aquarium and Cannery Row and I told you I had to go out of town and wouldn't see you for a while? Well, that wasn't exactly the truth. It was more than that, or I would never have stopped seeing you for so long."

"I know. You and Mom had a fight."

"She told you that?"

"No, but I could tell because she cried for a long time after. She wouldn't tell me what happened, but I knew it was pretty serious."

They stopped at a cyclone fence about halfway out the length of the ship that marked the end of the rebuilt section. The foamy surf crashed into an opening beyond the barrier where the ship had broken apart, causing the rusty rebar and chunks of broken concrete to quiver as each wave crashed into the *Palo Alto*'s hull.

"You're very grown-up for someone your age, Em, that's why I need to explain. I did something terrible that hurt your mom's feelings and caused her to not trust me. I guess I didn't realize just how important you and she were to me at the time, but I do now, and I'm trying to regain her trust and make it up to her—and to you. I hope she'll eventually agree to . . . well, you know what I mean."

"Be your girlfriend again?"

"If you think it's a bad idea, it's okay to tell me, I'll understand."

Emma looked up, then hugged him. "I'd like that a lot."

"You would?"

"I'll talk her into it if you want me to," she volunteered.

He squeezed her tight. "That's what I wanted to ask, if you'd help."

She clung for a few seconds, then let go and looked at him. "You've got tears in your eyes, Granz, are you crying?"

He rubbed his eyes with the sleeve of his T-shirt. "No, the darned wind makes my eyes water every time."

"Sure." She put her arm around his waist, and he drooped his on her shoulder. "Let's go so we have time to stop at Baskin-Robbins."

"Sounds like a good plan."

Later, as they drove up the steep road from the park, Emma said, "Dave, I really need to talk to Ashley about what to wear the first day of school. Are you sure you don't have your cell phone?"

He flipped open the glove box and handed her the phone. "Oh, there it is! I guess I was wrong earlier."

60

Dave and Emma snuggled beside each other on the sofa eating ice cream from the paper cartons. "Mom makes me use a bowl and only gives me one scoop," Emma said.

"Me, too," Dave told her, extending his elbow. "I won't tell if you won't."

She bumped her elbow against his twice. "Deal. Oh, there's Mom." Emma slurped on a spoon of ice cream and turned her attention to the television.

Larry stared into the camera, his huge dark eyes and red suspenders contrasting with the white backdrop. "This evening, my guest comes to you from the studio of KSAL, our affiliate station in Salinas, California. The entire hour will be devoted to issues surrounding missing and exploited children and, I warn you, what you are about to hear will shock you. But first, some good news."

The screen split to show Kathryn Mackay seated in the Salinas studio, then zoomed in on Mackay while King's voice-over announced, "With me tonight is Santa Rita County, California, District Attorney Kathryn Mackay. Ms. Mackay, thanks for being on the program."

"Thank you for having me. As you said, I do have some great news tonight. As a direct result of your June twelfth special telecast, Larry, we located one of the kidnapped infants and she is being returned to her parents."

The screen split again. "You're referring to Jane Alexander, the baby for whose return you appealed on this program?"

"That's right. Without your help, and your producer's, this wouldn't have been possible. And that's not all. I'm happy to announce that we have also recovered three other missing infants who are, at this very moment, safe and sound in the custody of Child Protective Services."

"Three? Counting Jane Alexander, that's four. Weren't five babies kidnapped?"

The screen shrank again and King and Mackay's images moved to the top, while photographs of Nathan Sweet, Martin Flowers and James Flynt scrolled slowly across the bottom. Under each photo, the infant's name and birth date appeared. "These are the infants we recovered, Larry." Mackay looked down briefly, then back into the camera. "Tragically, one of the infants didn't survive. We're withholding his identity at the request of the parents. I'm sure you understand."

King nodded. "Have these babies been returned to their parents yet?"

Mackay shook her head. "Not yet."

"Is that because they were sold on the black market to adoptive parents who don't want to give them up?"

Mackay tried, not completely successfully, to mask her surprise. "I'm sorry, but I can't comment on an ongoing investigation. The infants will stay in protective custody until the Court orders them returned."

"I see. What can you tell us about the circumstances surrounding their recovery? Have you identified the kidnappers?"

"All I can say at this time is that an arrest has been made and we are just beginning our investigation."

The camera pulled back to a full shot of King, with a small insert in the upper right corner of Mackay's face. "You'll keep the media informed?" he asked.

"Of course."

King peered into the camera as Mackay's image faded. "If what District Attorney Mackay told you was surprising, what I have to tell you next will shock you. In a copyrighted story, this morning's *New York Times* exposed an unbelievable connection between Long Island, New York and Agua Prieta, Mexico, a town just across the Arizona border, where families live in fly-infested shacks with dirt floors, and working women earn less than forty dollars a month."

Larry swung right to follow the camera. "Unless they have children. The *Times* reported that a Long Island lawyer and two accomplices have been arrested and charged with operating an international baby-smuggling ring that buys children for a few hundred dollars apiece in Agua Prieta, then sells them to American adoptive parents for as much as fifty thousand.

"Government officials report at least fifteen such illegal placements, although many of the adoptive parents claimed that they themselves were victims of a sleazy scheme that lured them into illegal agreements, and capitalized on their desperation to have children."

Larry paused. "Only time will tell how this baby stealing ring might be connected to the babies District Attorney Mackay recovered.

"After the commercial break, we'll interview a panel of experts on child abduction and parent grief counseling, then open up the phone lines and take your calls."

61

DEPARTMENT OF JUSTICE LABORATORY
MOTOR VEHICLE INSPECTION SECTION
MONDAY, JUNE 28, 10:15 A.M.

Granz swung the rented Buick into the Department of Justice complex at 46A Research Drive, nicknamed "Building 46" by law enforcement. A cyclone fence with strategically mounted security cameras protected the perimeter of the facility, which commanded an enviable view of the bay. A steep concrete driveway wrapped around the west side of the building and connected the street-side parking lot to a subterranean garage equipped to strip a vehicle down to the bare frame, piece-by-piece if necessary, to recover evidence.

Roselba Menendez met them wearing faded Levis and a blue T-shirt with a Mexico City Harley-Davidson logo on the front, and motioned with her finger. "Follow me around to the vehicle inspection area."

"How'd Los Gatos PD find it?"

"Luck. A homeowner complained about it being abandoned in front of his house, a couple of blocks from where Galbraith stole the Cherokee. It didn't have any license plates, he shined a flashlight inside and saw a set lying face up on the floor inside, and gave her the number. They came back to your name."

"The plates the bastard took the day he blew up your Explorer," Mackay added.

Menendez punched her personal identity code into an electronic panel, and waited while the computer validated the PIN, then the double metal doors rolled up to reveal a spotless three-car service bay.

A black Chevrolet Suburban sat on the hydraulic lift with all the doors open, wheels at eye level, and a tripod-mounted Pentax camera and bank of portable lights aimed at the right front wheel.

"The tow truck just unhooked it about an hour ago, but it has Bridgestone low-noise Duelers, size 245-70R-16, and the DOT number matches the tire tread impression from the Alexander crime scene. The right front tire exhibits distinctive road hazard and wear pattern characteristics, especially on several outer tread segments. They match the tire tread impression castings from the Alexander crime scene and the casting from near the dead infant's grave at Mt. Cabrillo."

Menendez led them to the right front of the Suburban, where she pointed to a number of V-shaped gouges, slices and nicks on the tire with a sharp-pointed, wood-handled awl and compared them to photographs of the dental stone castings.

"They typically result from running over objects on the roadway, small bits of metal, rocks, glass, or even something large like an old muffler, tailpipe, hubcap or something like that," Menendez explained. "It happens to all tires, but no two exhibit identical damage patterns."

"So, this tire definitely left both impressions?"

"Absolutely." She led them to a workbench and handed Granz a sealed, clear plastic evidence bag. "I found this pair of Nike Air Cross Trainers under the driver's seat. I haven't had time to compare them to the photographs Yamamoto took, but they're size twelve and I suspect they'll match."

"Anything else?" Mackay asked.

"I recovered fabric transfers from the rear seat upholstery. Mostly black, but there were a few pink cotton threads that could be—"

"From a baby blanket," Mackay volunteered.

Menendez nodded.

Mackay ran her fingers through her hair, then realized she had mussed it, and smoothed it down. "Galbraith already admitted he was involved. I'm not sure it adds a lot to have his car."

"That's what I thought, too," Menendez responded, handing them each a single sheet of paper. "I ran the Vehicle Identification Number through Motor Vehicles. The Suburban wasn't Galbraith's."

Mackay arched her eyebrows and looked up. "The VIN's registered to Ozark, Inc. in San Francisco."

"DMV records show a small fleet of Suburbans, six counting this one, registered to Ozark, Inc. SFPD patched me into the city's computerized Geologic Information System and business license databases. Business license records show no such company, but the GIS gave us something interesting. The address is a residential neighborhood. A condo to be exact.

Guess who the owner was—until it was sold recently."

Mackay crossed her arms over her chest, and waited, but knew better than to rush Menendez.

The criminalist handed Mackay the San Francisco GIS printout. "Robert Simmons," she said.

62

OFFICE OF DISTRICT ATTORNEY
KATHRYN MACKAY
MONDAY, JUNE 28, 1:15 P.M.

"We received Cellmark Lab's report," Granz said. "Jane Alexander/Amanda Manoff's DNA test results confirm her birth parents to be the couple in San Antonio. Her name's Tracy Ann Womack."

"The Manoffs sued for custody in federal court," Mackay reminded him.

Granz slid a sheet of paper across the desk. "This came by fax."

Mackay read it quickly. "The cover page of the Manoffs' filing—'dismissed with prejudice at request of plaintiffs.' They've dropped their custody suit. What about the Alexanders?"

Granz shook his head. "They aren't pursuing custody. Tracy Womack's going home. None of the adoptive parents intend to fight for custody, either. The head of Cellmark Labs promised to work around the clock until the DNA tests results are done, hopefully confirming their birth parents. They should all be home within a week."

"All except one," Mackay said softly.

Epilogue

At five after four, Kathryn's direct, private phone line rang.

"Hello?" she answered.

"Kathryn?" The man's voice sounded tinny and distant.

"Who is this?"

"Robert Simmons. It's good to hear your voice, Kate. I've missed you."

"You bastard, where are you?"

"Why so hostile, Kathryn?"

"We arrested Galbraith, and New York Police busted your East Coast accomplices. You're next."

He chuckled, but it was mirthless, closer to a sneer. "You seriously underestimate me, Kate, you always have. Shall I tell you how the New York Times *broke that story? I called them. They paid me handsomely for that exclusive story, wired a substantial deposit to my offshore account, then interviewed me by phone. I made a year's profit on that deal. Those fools in New York were expend-*

able, same as Galbraith. I'll use the Times money to start a new operation. Bigger, better, more lucrative."

There was a long silence before he continued. "I'm in Barcelona, Kathryn. Come for me if you wish, but I'll be gone. You'll never find me."

"I will eventually, count on it. You'll never draw another breath in peace," she promised, then she carefully placed the phone receiver into the cradle and drew in a deep breath.

Dave stared at her. "You're going to Spain?"

She shrugged.

"I thought we were making progress on a relationship, Kate. You're putting your obsession with Simmons ahead of you and me and your other duties. Not to mention Emma. I can't promise I'll be available when you get back."

"I know."

More to relish from

CHRISTINE McGUIRE

Until We Meet Again

Until the Bough Breaks

Until Death Do Us Part

Until Proven Guilty

Until the Day They Die

Available from Pocket Books

2351-01

Visit
❖ Pocket Books ❖
online at

www.SimonSays.com

Keep up on the latest new releases from your favorite authors, as well as author appearances, news, chats, special offers and more.

2381-01